MISFIT LIL HIDES OUT

Lieutenant-General George Hamilton Morgan has been sent by Washington to ensure the elimination of the Apache Angry-fist, and his delinquent bucks' reign of terror. Misfit Lil, believing his arrival to be a slur on Colonel Brook Lexborough and her friends at Fort Dennis, speaks her mind, little realising the consequence of her plain talking. Then as murder intervenes, and incriminating evidence is found in Lil's saddlebag, she heads for the hills — and into danger!

CHAP O'KEEFE

MISFIT LIL
HIDES OUT

Complete and Unabridged

LINFORD
Leicester

First published in Great Britain in 2008 by
Robert Hale Limited
London

First Linford Edition
published 2009
by arrangement with
Robert Hale Limited
London

British Library CIP Data

O'Keefe, Chap.
  Misfit Lil hides out - -
  (Linford western library)
  1. Apache Indians- -Fiction. 2. Western stories.
  3. Large type books.
  I. Title II. Series
  823.9'14–dc22

ISBN 978–1–84782–739–5

Published by
F. A. Thorpe (Publishing)
Anstey, Leicestershire

Set by Words & Graphics Ltd.
Anstey, Leicestershire
Printed and bound in Great Britain by
T. J. International Ltd., Padstow, Cornwall

This book is printed on acid-free paper

1

Unheeded Warning

The reservation jumpers led by Angry-he-shakes-fist were on the warpath. The mounted string of young delinquents wore only breech-clouts or leggings and their smooth, bronze bodies glistened with oil and medicine paint.

Angry-fist himself — whose riding style was especially distinctive since he'd lost his left hand in a tomahawk duel with the white scout Jackson Farraday — was decked out with a showy, plumed war bonnet.

So much, Lilian Goodnight, daughter of the owner of the Flying G, biggest spread in the Silver Vein country, took in with one startled glance as she topped a jagged ridge on the edge of the canyonlands.

'Warpath' was too grand a word for

Angry-fist's activities, Lil thought, correcting her swift impression. The armed braves she saw through heat shimmers, winding across a grey-brown plain dotted with clusters of rock and sagebrush, were effectively a murderous gang of young criminals under the leadership of a charismatic hothead who'd grown increasingly bitter and twisted. Chanting a ululating deathsong, the riders formed a raiding party of thugs out to strike terror for amusement and to grab plunder for reward.

Still in early womanhood, but a veteran of frontier hardship and survival, Lil knew she'd be skylined if any of the painted killers should look up. She quickly drew back. Angry-fist's ruffiantly bunch had clashed with her before. The bucks would welcome the diverting thrill of hunting down 'girl-who-shoots-fast'.

Far be it for them to know she was no model of virtue herself; that she'd been largely disowned by a vexed father unable to understand the waywardness of a child who'd been offered every available luxury but been seduced by the freedoms enjoyed by her often fiddlefooted male contemporaries to become Silver Vein's Princess of Pistoleers and more.

She was a broadminded girl with no prejudices against black people, Mexicans, Chinese, the poor . . . or Indians. But these renegades would chase, catch, rob, rape and kill regardless of where the victim's sympathies might lie.

Lil was touching spurless heels to her trusty grey cow-pony's ribs, breaking him into a trot, before she was hit by the significance of the direction in which Angry-fist's bunch was headed.

'Damn it!' she said out loud.

In a draw that sloped on to the plain some miles distant was a spring-fed pasture, an oasis of luxuriant green. The isolated pocket of fertility had attracted a couple from Colorado, Daniel and Edith Kennedy, who'd migrated further west on glowing letters of advice from

Dan's brother to stake out a claim.

The brother, Thomas Kennedy, served in the Army with the rank of corporal and as a member of the force garrisoned at Fort Dennis yonder from the township of Silver Vein. Tom's wife, Fanny, was one of the women at the fort with whom Lil had struck up a casual friendship.

Lil had last seen Fanny not shopping in the stores in town on some past day, but that very morning riding a solitary trail to her civilian in-laws' cabin to visit with them. Plainly, the local military were unaware Angry-fist was up to his old tricks in this neck of the woods.

The girls had stopped for several minutes to talk. Neither was a gossip but both led their lives as loners, though in dissimilar ways.

Had anyone witnessed the meeting they would have been struck by the contrasts between the two young women. For Lil was tall and slim, and very lithe. She was animated, with grey eyes of a peculiar brilliance that lit her brown face, and full of the zest for living. Fanny, on the other hand, was a reserved person of average build, without Lil's height or her natural exuberance and colour. Her hair was reddish but lacking in life where Lil's was glossy black and lengthy with a bit of curl and bounce.

Fanny Kennedy's life was not a chosen one. The dreariness of her existence in married enlisted men's quarters was taking a toll on her. Fort Dennis tittle-tattle had it little love was lost between Fanny and Tom in an age when a woman stood by her man, no matter what, especially when it provided her security in a harsh land. Moreover, the Kennedys were Catholics. Thought of a dissolution of their marriage would be as horrifying as it was impractical.

Lil's life was, conversely, the one she'd chosen and best enjoyed. Riding the wild country was hugely preferable over being the lady her long-suffering pa had had a mind for his tomboy daughter to become. It was Ben Goodnight's unwise insistence on enrolling her as a boarder at a high-toned seminary in Boston, from which she'd subsequently been expelled after unacceptable, after-hours behaviour involving an eagerly co-operative gardener's-boy, that had earned Miss Lilian the sobriquet of Misfit Lil. She and genteel Boston hadn't hitched up alongside one another at all.

Clad in pants and buckskin tunic fringed in the style of an old-time mountain man, Lil now strived to emulate her idol, Jackson Farraday, the hugely experienced, weather-burnished frontiersman who made his livelihood as a guide and a civilian scout for the army.

Lil found Fanny nervy but likeable. She suspected Fanny found her odd and shocking, but she hoped they could be friends. She didn't subscribe to the belief that Tom Kennedy gave his wife a hard time — some said he beat her — and suspected an additional reason

6

Kennedy had lured his brother and sister-in-law into the territory might be to make supportive kinfolks available to Fanny.

'Nice day for riding,' Lil had said not two hours previous.

'That it is,' Fanny had responded shyly to Silver Vein's notorious female saddle-tramp.

'Where are you going?' Lil had prompted, though she could guess.

'I'm going to visit with Edith and Dan at their homestead. Their mare has foaled.' Fanny had raised a smile. 'Edith sent us a note saying the colt's really cute and to come see him soon. She plans to raise and train him her ownself.'

Lil had slapped her grey's neck approvingly. 'Why, that's just what I did with ol' Rebel here. It paid off. He'll do about anything for me.'

Now Rebel was going to have to go like the wind. For it fell to Lil to take swift word to the Kennedys of their peril as hell-bent red renegades rode for their pleasant valley.

'They're devils — cold, cruel, killing devils — that's what they are,' Lil grumbled to herself. Dan Kennedy was making a mistake trying to prove up in such a lonesome place, desirable and peaceable though it might look. Since Angry-fist had broken out of the reservation, it wasn't safe. A man did wrong bringing his woman to live there.

Lil reined the game bronc on to no known trail. By heading across broken terrain, she could get to the Kennedy's cabin before the raiders. But though she knew the country like the back of her hand as few others did, the route was difficult, dangerous. It needed all her skills as a rider and the sure-footedness of her mount. One false step, one misplaced hoof, could bring death by accident to either or both of them — and spell slaughter without warning for the three Kennedys.

Travelling at a pace that didn't allow for second thoughts or calculating chances, she nonetheless picked a way up mountainously steep slopes where only scrub oak and dwarf pinon grew. She wondered all the while whether any of Angry-fist's crowd had spied her and set out to run her down. Any moment she feared she'd hear the crack of a rifle or the zing of an arrow.

Eventually, to reach the Kennedy place coming this way, she would have to cross a breathtakingly deep ravine. It was part of her daring tactics. Rebel, she figured, would make the leap. But for any pursuing Indians on half-wild mustangs, it would be a near-impossible feat. Their mounts, though fleet-footed, were smaller and less well cared for and trained.

Foolhardy though some of Angry-fist's followers might be, they would think more than twice before attempting the jump. A slip, a split-second of mistiming, would hurl them to a bone-smashing death in the shadowed, rocky depths far below.

Lil set Rebel on a straight run for the edge to the chasm. The gap and the sheer wall of vertically stratified red rock that was its far side came into sudden view when it was already too late to check or turn aside.

Lil strived to keep the flutters in her own nervous stomach from conveying themselves to her intelligent horse. She knew she was tossing their lives on the hazard.

'Good boy, you can do it!' she murmured encouragingly, knowing it was now all up to him.

The horse and Lil understood one another completely. With a tremendous thrust of his powerful legs, Rebel launched them into the air. They soared.

For seconds nothing was below them but an expanse of hot, trapped air and the distant, jagged upthrusts of rock from a dry and barren floor laid in an aeon past by a savage nature with no thought of the advent of puny man. Its configurations were so violent, its access so precarious, it might never have been trod by human feet.

Then Rebel's front hoofs hit the far

side, sending loose rock rolling. In a wild scramble of crumbling particles from the very edge of the rim, his rear hoofs gained a purchase, too.

They were across!

Lil felt the sweat trickling from her armpits. Least I didn't wet myself, she thought. And they were thundering on, Lil letting the astute cow pony pick his own way.

'Attaboy, Reb! We made it!' she cried exultantly.

The remaining mile was eaten up lickety-spit. The Kennedy claim came in to sight — a modest barn, a horse shed and a log cabin with a stone chimney but otherwise only the barest accommodations within. All three had sheet-iron corrugated roofs. The shed had a roof sloping one way with the high part to the south. It was fully enclosed on three sides but most the south side was open and Lil glimpsed Fanny's mount hitched alongside the Kennedys' mare and her tiny, spindly-legged colt.

Lil rode down into the yard between the buildings. After his great-hearted effort, Rebel was showing signs of fatigue, but Lil slipped from saddle to ground, paying no attention to his needs outside of leaving him heading for a water trough.

A young black dog frisked from behind the barn, barking excitedly. The Kennedys came out to check on the sudden arrival and outbreak of commotion.

Fanny was the last through the door but first to speak.

'Why are you here, Lil?' she asked, puzzled but sensing something was wrong. 'What's happened?'

'It's the Apache renegades!' Lil blurted breathlessly. 'They're coming to raid this place. You've got to grab your valuables and get out fast!'

She knew their transportable belongings would be meagre and they had saddle horses as well as a buckboard.

But Dan Kennedy — stockily built and of a bullish breed that stood its ground — was far from convinced. He said pugnaciously, 'I don't know 'bout that, missy. I figure a big scattergun plumb loaded with buckshot is the way to greet sich varmints.'

'A few dead 'uns won't put off these hotheads,' Lil said. 'There's too many of 'em. Most everyone hereabouts knows there's no stopping Angry-fist's raiding parties once their blood is up. They're mean. They're cruel. They're killers. You've got to ride!'

'Oh, Dan!' Edith cried, stricken and disbelieving. 'We'll lose everything we've worked for — '

She was a mature woman who'd expended the beauty and strength of her prime on the challenge of setting up here. She'd laboured as hard as any man though there was little about her that looked male.

'No, we won't. Get inside, close the shutters, woman — we're gonna fight!'

Appalled, Lil said, 'Tell them, Fanny! That's playing a mighty, mighty dangerous game. It won't work. We've got to get away now, to the fort. Please!'

But Fanny clenched her raised hands, nervously and undecided. She said nothing. Her face was white and her tongue seemingly frozen.

'No red heathens mess with Dan Kennedy, gal!' the homesteader growled at Lil. 'I got the guns and plenty o' cartridges. Either you stay an' help or light a shuck on your own.'

Lil choked back rising anger. She swallowed the further protests she'd no time to deliver.

'All right, I will! Fanny — get your hoss and ride out with me. Don't see a lick of sense in your Corporal Tom being made a widower to boot.'

Lil strode over to Rebel and jumped astride.

Fanny dithered, turning one way then the other, while her kin hurried back into the cabin. As though making up her mind, she rushed after Edith and Dan.

'Hey, Fanny!' Lil yelled. 'Ain't you coming with me?'

Fanny crossed the cabin's threshold. Dan immediately took down a repeating rifle from wall pegs and thrust it into her hands.

'It's fully loaded. Sixteen shots,' he said.

She looked down at the weapon, horrified.

'I can't — I don't — I won't . . . '

She shuddered and looked over her shoulder for Lil.

Misfit Lil's reputation for knowing what she was about in such situations was a local legend, heard in army barracks as in every other place. Seeing Lil about to head off, and having shaky confidence at best in her brother-in-law, Fanny changed her mind again.

'Don't leave me, Lil! I'm coming with you!'

She ran out to the barn and her horse, still clutching the rifle like she didn't want it, or know what she was going to do with it, but it had somehow become glued to her hands.

Behind, the cabin door was slammed

and a stout bar thudded into place back of it. In the yard. Lil took the burden of the rifle off Fanny and the young army wife rose into her saddle.

The pair rode out quickly. Lil was determined to be out of sight before Angry-fist's bunch arrived. But she felt bad about leaving the Kennedy couple to fight off the coming Indian attack. How could people be so stupid?

'Curse 'em for pigheaded green-horns!' she gritted as they slanted out of the grassy bottom. They headed for the front, rising bench of the rough country that walled in the Kennedys' valley. Here, Lil knew she could find them concealment.

Lil had a carbine in a scabbard under her left leg, but she rode with Fanny's rifle in her hand, half laid across her thighs. When she reached the first jumble of rocky outcrops, she slowed and swore.

'Aw, hell, it's damned foolishness, but I can't quit this easy and Rebel's already gotten in a lather once today.

We'll stop and see what happens . . . help if we can.'

Fanny's mount, though a docile creature, had got caught up in the excitement of their rapid flight. It fell to Lil to reach out and grab the bridle as the horse surged past. The rifle from the Kennedys slipped to the ground with a clatter, her arm was almost tugged from its socket and she was nearly jerked from the saddle.

'Lil!' Fanny sobbed. 'What are you doing? Leave go of my bridle!'

But Lil and Rebel were a strong combination and were able to pull them into the cover of a huge boulder from where they could observe the Kennedy ranch from a position on the steep overlooking slope only hundreds of yards distant as a crow might fly.

Lil swung an athletic leg over Rebel's neck and dropped down. 'Fetch your rifle,' she snapped.

Fanny stared at her, white and trembling. 'I don't want it! Didn't we ought to ride on?'

'Too late for that. They'd spot us. Look!'

Her pointing finger turned Fanny's fearful attention to a cloud of dust thrown up by a string of savage riders on fleet ponies. They had rounded a stark granite bluff and were into the green valley, bearing down fast on the Kennedys' placid spread with patently sinister purpose.

'They're plumb on top of the place now!'

Fanny turned away as though denying the spectacle. Her back and arms stiffened and her hands formed fists. The girl was on the point of breaking down.

'I don't want to see it! I don't want to see it!'

2

Valley of Death

In choosing to fight it out with Angry-fist's criminal band, Dan and Edith Kennedy were gambling their lives. To Lil's mind, they were throwing them away as recklessly as any pay-day cowboy suckered into slapping his full month's forty-dollar roll on a saloon table in front of a professional, black-coated card-cheat.

Dan took first blood. As soon as the first renegade came within a hundred yards of the cabin, he tumbled him from his mustang's back with a rifle shot that turned a six-inch patch of his bronze shoulder into red mincemeat.

The redmen drew off beyond range, then began circling the cabin, some clockwise, some anti-clockwise. They whooped and hurled taunts at the

19

confused white pair who never knew quite when a hostile would cross a field of fire encompassed by one slit or another beside the cabin's stoutly fixed shutters.

Lil's heart leaped gladly when a rebel Apache's bronc stopped a slug in the chest and folded under him.

'That's it, Dan Kennedy! Show the red devils!'

But she knew it was all bravado and the couple couldn't hold out.

Angry-fist was maddened by the preparedness of the whites in their isolated homestead. He gave a signal for his bucks to fall back. Even as they retreated, a pair of carbines barked viciously from the cabin and a third raider stopped lead. He reeled and sagged, pulling his mount's head round and smashing into the pony of the brother in hell-raising pounding alongside. They hit the ground locked together in a dust-raising, bone-breaking cartwheel of animal and human limbs.

Lil was a crackshot and from the

safety of the girls' hiding place she debated with herself whether she should put her carbine — or better, Dan Kennedy's rifle — to use and pick off some of the raiding party herself.

'Your in-laws' lives are at stake. Think I should kill one or two myself?' she mused aloud.

Fanny blurted, 'No! They'd figure it wasn't done from the cabin. Out here, we'd have less of a chance than Dan and Edith. We'd never get clear!'

Lil realized she was right. Sure, she could take her pot-shots, and be reasonably confident in her skill to lessen the odds minimally. But whether it would avail themselves or the pair in the cabin more was questionable. The girls' position would be betrayed, and the Indians would have two extra potential victims to harry to gruesome deaths.

When Angry-fist resumed his attack, he'd re-thought his tactics. A shower of arrows winged across the brilliant blue sky toward the cabin, trailing black smoke and red fire.

'Double damn!' Lil said. 'They aim to burn 'em out!'

The burning arrows flopped on to the roof. Others found the shutters and lodged in the chinks of the back wall. The smoke and smell of smouldering timber drifted to Lil and Fanny on the breeze. Inside the cabin it would quickly become a choking hell.

The crackle of long guns' fire broke out again from the cabin, but the Indians held back, tormentingly out of range. And they shot more fiery arrows at every nook and cranny in the exposed timber.

As a small blaze took hold to the left of the front door, an impetuous buck could restrain himself no longer and stormed the cabin, yelling bastardized war-cries. Lil took a chance, got him in the rifle's sights and shot him clean off his scraggy cayuse's back. In the crackle of flames and the Kennedys' own gunfire, the direction her almost-spent bullet came from went unnoticed. But the buck lurched to his feet, spilling blood and brandishing a tomahawk.

He smashed at the door. Splinters flew and planks parted, opening the way before a bullet from within took him full in the chest. He expelled the last air in his lungs in a hideous death scream. He plunged through the remnants of the door and it was left gaping.

The draught created fanned the flames to fresh fury. They burst through the roof buckling the sheet iron, part of which fell in, and Dan and Edith came stumbling out of their breached stronghold blindly.

Dan fired the gun in his hands at random, repeatedly, swinging it in all directions through the billowing black smoke but hitting nothing.

Lil tried to sight on the laughing redmen who rushed in for the kill, but at such a distance she dared not fire on the mêlée for fear of hitting Dan or his wife.

Then it was too late. A thrown axe

cleaved Dan's skull, ending his life instantly, pitching him headlong and silent into the dust of his yard.

Unseeing, Edith floundered into the eager, waiting hands of the five young mongrels who quickly fell on her. She struggled, screamed and kicked as they dragged her away from the smoky hell toward a grassy bank.

Lil knew what was going to happen. Again, she was powerless to stop it. Fanny was no use either, She'd collapsed into a quivering wreck, hiding her face in her hands and whispering what sounded like terror-fraught prayers punctuated with sobs.

Despite their ribald excitement, the five who'd grabbed Edith worked efficiently and swiftly. With yips and grunts, their claw-like hands tore at her clothes, ripping them apart at the seams, hooking knives through her undergarments.

Lil watched the awful spectacle unfold, anguished by her inability to intervene. Edith's torturers mocked her plight.

Two men held her ankles, lifting them; another pinned her shoulders to the ground. One clapped a hand over her mouth and nose to stifle her shrieks. The fifth man, a huge bear of a brave, released leather thongs securing his leggings and twisted his breechclout to one side. The muscles in his copper-coloured back rippled. Ruthlessly, Edith was solidly pinned by the determined intrusion. And being additionally restrained by his accomplices, she was unable so much as to squirm. On a gargantuan heave of indrawn breath, the buck went rigid on top of her.

Either Edith must have bitten the hand of the man gagging her, or he relaxed his grip. For the homesteader's wife was able to let out a piercing, chilling cry. From the depth of her tortured being it conveyed to her two hidden and civilized sisters the woman's extreme horror and revulsion.

Lil was momentarily beside herself with frustration. Without the confusion of gunfire from the cabin, any shot she fired could be guaranteed to imperil Fanny's life and hers, let alone Edith's. What should she do?

The problem was resolved before she could think of any suitable action. When the first Indian rolled off their victim, and while the others were jostling to be next to violate her. Edith retched and threw up over the man who'd muffled her screams.

'Waugh!' he grunted, his nose wrinkling and his lip curling with distaste.

The soiled buck was furious. With a howl of rage, he pulled a long knife from a sheath at his hip and plunged it forcefully and deep into Edith's breast. '*Die, filth*!'

His anger brought an abrupt and merciful end to Edith's ravishing and her life. It also brought consternation among his cheated comrades. They began gabbling remonstrations that escalated rapidly into grappling and an exchange of blows.

Fire was engulfing the cabin, threatening to spread to the outbuildings. The rest of the raiding party crowded round Edith's foiled rapists and murderer, yelling encouragement to their sparring. Lil was decided: time would never be better to quit the confused and ugly scene.

'C'mon, Fanny! You've got to snap out of it. Your in-laws are dead and beyond our help. There's nothing we can do just now and we need to make ourselves scarce fast, before those rotten devils lose interest in their pickings.'

Rebel was right alongside her. She clutched at his bridle, turning him round, and vaulted into the saddle. To her relief, Fanny pulled herself together sufficiently to follow her example and mount up.

Bent low, keeping out of sight behind the bulk of the rock that had given them concealment, they rode as hard as they could; rode off into the fringes of the maze of canyonlands where most men would be lost.

Lil knew the canyonlands' twists and

turns — their barren, unforgiving magnificence — inside out. Angry-fist did also. But Lil figured she'd given him no reason to be looking for them. So far . . .

At last they were able to sit up straight and look down their backtrail. Reassuringly, it was free of any tell-tale banner of dust or echo of hoofbeats that might be the first sign of pursuit.

Lil feared Fanny was close to cracking up again. She was shaking terribly and with towering brown walls of heat-blasted rock closing around them with every step, they were in no place where anybody should be shivering.

'I can't stand any more. Why have we come here?' Fanny asked in a small voice. 'It's awful. I want to go back to the fort.'

'So you shall,' Lil said. 'When it's safe to head thataway. For now, you've got me with you as your friend.'

Lil wasn't so sure of herself as to add she was a hard-riding, gun-handy gal who knew her way around and could stand between Fanny and the heap of trouble she'd landed in. She'd already saved their own scalps, hadn't she?

She did appreciate how intimidatingly bleak the surroundings would be to a person not used to them. Despite the glaring brightness and the heat, Fanny had witnessed the sounds if not the sight of the slaughter of kin folks. Any strange place she was taken into immediately after would have taken on the atmosphere of a black nightmare.

Lil's plan was a basic one. They'd wait for nightfall when the renegade Apaches would have left the Kennedy property. Then it would be time to return, cautiously. The moon would be better than half-full and bright tonight and Lil would do what she could to bury the Kennedys' broken bodies.

After that, she'd have to escort Fanny back to Fort Dennis, where no doubt some concern would be felt in due course about the failure of Corporal Tom Kennedy's wife to return from her ride.

And if she could fit it in, she thought daringly, she might track the raiding party to its night camp and work at least a few tricks of vengeance on the sleeping Indians . . .

But that would be breathtakingly audacious play.

★　★　★

Smoke drifted upward lazily from the blackened shell of the Kennedys' cabin and formed a flat layer in the grey night sky. Fallen beams and the iron roof still held a dim red glow. The air was acrid.

Neither of the girls had Bible or Prayer Book, but Lil did find a strong, sharp-bladed spade in the Kennedys' unburned horse shed, though the Indians had stolen the mare and her cute foal.

Lil was tall and lean and her muscles were in athletic trim. But digging a grave, albeit in soft, good valley-bottom earth, wasn't as easy or quick a job as popular supposition had it. Lil had grown up on the frontier where life was tough and grim. As a child in a motherless, male environment on the Flying G, she'd seen how such chores were done despite her father's best efforts to shield her from the harsh realities of life, of which death was one.

'We can't leave their bodies for the coyotes and other scavenging varmints,' she told Fanny. 'I'm strong for a girl. I'll do the digging. You make us the crosses for when I'm done.'

She didn't expect or want the traumatized woman to see at close hand what had happened to the Kennedys. Angry-fist's hellions had made deft incisions and peeled away their scalps, exposing redly clotted bone where black flies now crawled.

Dan Kennedy's body had been plundered of all but underwear. Edith's naked remains were also minus her full breasts and the hair and portion between her legs. When the swarms of flies could be prevailed upon to rise sporadically from their feast, Lil could see sharp knives and a degree of neat, surgical skill had been put to evil use.

'That's foul,' she muttered. 'Why would they want such trophies?'

In fact, she knew. A drunken soldier had once offered her, more to shock than seriously, loot that had comprised several pouches made recognizably from the cured skin of women's body parts.

What had been done to Edith before and after her death strengthened Lil's resolve to claim at least several more token lives from Angry-fist's band with the least delay.

The gravedigging was no easier than she'd expected. Burying the dead was an ugly, cheerless job. The dirt got into her hair, nostrils and mouth. And in the end, she didn't dig to the full depth she would have liked, knowing she had other tasks she wanted to attend to, She decided to compensate by piling heavy rocks on to the mound of the grave.

Finally, when the bodies were under the ground and the girls had whispered extempore prayers over the finished grave, Lil persuaded Fanny to rest some in the shed. She didn't mention her own back, shoulders and arms ached; that she was feeling sweaty and filthy.

'I'll go back with you to Fort Dennis at first light.'

'I'm not much use for a soldier's wife, am I?' Fanny said tearfully. 'Not much help. At least you shot one of the fiends. I'm sorry I was such a ninny. I've always been that way . . . Well, maybe not always, but since I was a very small child. My parents and brothers were massacred by the Cheyenne in Colorado. I was the sole survivor. I don't think I've ever gotten properly over it. I think about what happened often, ask myself why, though I know the answer. And I still have nightmares about it.'

'Oh, I'm sorry . . . I didn't know,' Lil said awkwardly. 'All this . . . *wickedness* must have brought it back to you real bad.'

Fanny nodded slowly. 'But I have to

confess, I'm very different from you, Lil. When I heard this Angry-fist and his killers were coming, I went into a complete funk. I didn't know which way to turn; what I should do. I felt near paralysis when Dan handed me the rifle.'

'Well, you're safe here for now. I don't think Angry-fist will come back this way in a hurry. He's shrewd enough to know there'll be big trouble over what his gang has done here.'

Tentatively, Lil broached the next part of her plan.

'I could go scout out where the murdering bunch has taken itself off . . . ' She didn't dare hint at her intention to take even small-scale reprisals.

Fanny's face again became a sheet of white paper on which an artist had scratched a stark drawing of miserable fear with the black strokes of a pen.

'I'd rather you stayed.'

'You'll be all right here, I tell you. You mustn't be scared.'

'Wh-what if you — you don't get back?'

Lil laughed with a deal more poise than she felt.

'I can look after myself all right! Anyway, the soldiers are plumb sure to come looking for you tomorrow, seeing that you never returned to the fort.'

She flicked her tongue across her dry lips, tasting the fine soot that permeated the air from the smouldering cabin. It was no good omen for what she was choosing to do. For it seemed to hold the unpalatable, bitter taste of death.

3

Find That Woman!

Jackson Farraday was fetched by a trooper to Fort Dennis. The land to the sharp edge of the horizon was growing dark and the orange of sunset was fading higher up into pale gold. The deceptive calm of the short, swift twilight was on the land, but Jackson knew a pressing matter must be on the mind of Colonel Brook Lexborough.

Why else would the fort's commanding officer have summoned him at an hour when light was failing?

Since Jackson had a deep respect for Colonel Lexborough, he was himself gripped by a sense of the urgency for which he didn't know the cause.

The massive wooden gates swung to behind the arriving pair on groaning hinges. Fort Dennis was a mix of log blockhouses — housing the men's barracks, the stables, a blacksmith's shop and the mess shack — and stone structures. The latter included an administration block, officers' quarters, the infirmary, a commissary and the guardhouse — all evidence to the availability of rock nearby and masons' skills.

Jackson left the trooper to tend their mounts. He strode across the wide, level parade ground to the administration building.

He was every inch a frontiersman. He was imposingly tall with long, sun-bleached hair and a neat chin beard — an all-seasons-hardened civilian scout and guide who worked when occasion required for the army.

In the past, he'd hunted buffalo and supplied meat for railroad construction workers. He'd also carried dispatches through hostile Indian country. But he had most in common with the pathfinders who'd blazed western trails earlier in the century. An educated man, he reputedly spoke seven languages plus an assortment of Indian dialects. He subscribed to the beliefs of the visionary explorer and lobbyist John Wesley Powell, who promoted scientific survey and the rational use of the West's resources.

Recently, Jackson had been in the Henrys as guide to a geologist conducting a study of the unique volcanic features of the Unknown Mountains — for such Powell himself had originally called the remote range before returning two years later to name it after Joseph Henry, a friend and the secretary of the Smithsonian Institution.

Tonight, Jackson's sure step carried him into a bare corridor where his bootfalls echoed ringingly. He rapped the panels of a door at the far end with his knuckles.

'Come in!' a deep voice boomed.

Jackson entered.

'Ah, Mr Farraday. Much obliged to you for coming. I fear we're going to need your services, and promptly.'

'Trouble brewing, Colonel?'

'It might be, and at the worst possible juncture.'

The colonel uncoiled himself from a cramped position behind a scarred and paper-littered desk and came forward to shake Jackson's hand.

He was a big man — tall, heavy-built — in his late fifties. He had crinkled, iron-grey hair and a piercing gaze that suggested not much escaped his notice. When Jackson was seated, he returned to his own creaking swivel chair, crossed his long legs to one side, and came to business quickly.

'There's a woman missing — one of the enlisted men's wives who live here at the fort, and I'm assured by Geraldine, who keeps track of these affairs — who notes such things — that it would be out of character for her to have absconded.'

Jackson arched a brow enquiringly. 'And the rest?' He knew that Lexborough must have more bothering him than his wife's concern over one soldier's missing wife.

The colonel took no offence at his tone. 'Quite right, Mr Farraday. There are somewhat larger considerations involved. They centre on our bothersome old enemy, Angry-he-shakes-fist.'

'That renegade has lived a charmed life since he defected from the reservation,' Jackson said, his face clouding. 'It can't last forever.'

Lexborough sighed gustily. 'And we don't have forever! Pens are scratching and tongues are wagging in places far afield. Fort Dennis is in danger of being held to account, and this woman's disappearance comes at an especially unfortunate juncture. If Angry-fist is revealed to be back of Fanny Kennedy's disappearance, it will fan some disagreeable flames.'

'Hmm. Do tell more, Colonel.'

Lexborough paused to drag down a deeper breath. Though he was on the best of terms with Jackson, and a blunt man to boot, he was a professional soldier and it didn't come easy for him to speak of matters in a way that might seem critical of the service.

He harrumphed and began.

'It's a nasty, complicated business. As you know, it has long been Washington's policy that we shouldn't come down too hard on Indians defecting from the reservations.'

Jackson nodded, knowing better than many that delinquent young redmen frequently had cause.

'But some eastern newspaper jasper passed through here,' Lexborough rumbled on. 'He observed Angry-fist was still at large after many months, occasionally looting and burning isolated pockets of white population as the mood took him. The journalist yapped something fierce, calling on Washington to demand action from its men in the field. It was a scandal, a disgrace and so forth. Terms like 'bloody rebellion' and 'making a mockery of the US Army' appeared in the popular prints. Washington wasn't happy, I wasn't happy.'

'I take it this newspaper dude had the ear of folks in high places,' Jackson said questioningly. 'That it has become a political issue.'

'Exactly, Mr Farraday. The War Department has advised that at the next hint of trouble, should there be one, these renegade Indians are to be eliminated. Furthermore, the meddling journalist suggested a need existed for someone from the army's general staff to leave Washington, come out here and take command of the situation. It has been taken up.'

'I'm indeed sorry to hear that, Colonel. It sounds like a withdrawal of trust.'

'We're to have a desk soldier on our backs,' Lexborough said sourly. 'Privately and frankly, one of the worst.'

Inwardly, Jackson shuddered. 'Will I have heard of him?'

'Probably not. I've come across him only the once myself. He has no lengthy record of active service, but he's well connected. Lieutenant-General George

Hamilton Morgan by rank and name.'

Jackson frowned. 'Means nothing to me.'

'That doesn't surprise me. He's a strutting man. full of self-importance who I can understand will be delighted to oversee the mission earmarked for him. His career and public profile plainly call for him to assume command of some suitable campaign in the field to augment victories in the corridors of power. He has a reputation in society as a womanizer and he fancies himself as a ladies' man, but you can make only limited capital out of such things. Hence his ambition to come West.'

'I get the picture, Colonel. You and your men do the work, take all the criticism and risks of failure, and this General Morgan takes any credit.'

'I believe so. The expedition will be a showpiece mission to placate and impress the Eastern newspapers. The benefit accrues to the general and his political friends, who paint all Indians as criminals and vermin.'

Jackson pondered, fitting together what he'd learned.

'So if Fanny Kennedy's disappearance becomes a matter of abduction by a resurgent Angry-fist, I take it this will be interpreted as sufficient cause to unleash General Morgan and the wrath of the white man.'

'That's about right, Mr Farraday. Mrs Kennedy was reported to have gone visiting with her in-laws, Dan and Edith Kennedy, who've settled in an isolated valley on the edge of the canyonlands.'

The 'Kennedy' name in this connection rang a bell in Jackson's memory.

'Ah . . . yes, I remember the couple you speak of. Against best advice, I believe.'

The colonel nodded gravely. 'If Angry-fist has raided their place, Morgan's tour and the campaign will be all on — instantly. The political will has been put in place, It merely waits for the pulling of a trigger. The only way it can be squared away, as I see it, is if we find Corporal Tom

Kennedy's wife or she turns up, and if the settler Kennedys are safe.'

'Well, I hope for everyone's sake this will be the case.'

Lexborough thumped his desk with the base of a clenched fist.

'Tomorrow, at first light, I want you to accompany a reconnaissance detail led by Lieutenant Michael Covington. The job will be to seek out what you can — read the signs, large or small. Unless everything is hunky-dory, unless we find that young woman, Mr Farraday, all hell is going to be let loose around us!'

★   ★   ★

Misfit Lil headed south by moonlight to a desolate place where the ground lifted in a circular rise, forming the brim of a basin. Artefacts she'd unearthed there on past explorations had shown her the inner hollow had been a site favoured by passing Indians in generations gone by.

Hell, she was determined to give Angry-fist and his braves some grief!

After several months lying low, the defectors from the reservation had killed two more white settlers, stolen their livestock and burned their house. Lil was in a tough, grim mood. The thought that her actions might be folly didn't so much as cross her unusual mind.

The smell of smoke from fires confirmed her hunch that the basin was where Angry-fist and his party had chosen to camp for the night, to boast among themselves of their prowess and to savour their booty. A small consolation was that Dan and Edith Kennedy no longer had to be considered. Both were beyond the torment they would have suffered had they lived to be dragged here and made part of the reprobates' festivities.

Lil took Rebel to where coarse grass grew under oaks at the foot of the basin's outer slopes. She tethered the horse and, armed with the Kennedys'

Winchester, sneaked back to spy on the Indians.

The light of their fires showed Lil they'd butchered the Kennedys' mare and her colt and gorged themselves on the meat. Many were now soundly asleep.

The first step was to spook their mounts, which in Lil's considered opinion were considerably less impressive horseflesh than what they'd lately consumed. The critters were mostly what she classed as scrub mustangs, fleet of foot and hardy, but because they'd responded poorly to training of the inferior kind the renegades were apt to spare them, they were highly strung and ready to jump at the slightest provocation.

Lil had known Indians to secure their horses from straying with hobbles of braided buffalo hide. But Angry-fist's mongrels, arrogantly confident of their security, had contained the animals by hitching them together through their crude halters and anchoring the rope to

47

an immovable boulder.

The first part was the riskiest. She had to reach the horses without causing a disturbance and slash the rope.

She put down the rifle and shifted a knife in its fringed sheath to the back of her belt. She slithered down the slope into the hollow on her belly, never raising her head higher than the long grass. Like a real, honest-to-God Indian, she thought wryly.

High overhead, the half-moon cast slanting rays of silver light into the basin and she could see the mustang herd plainly enough.

One of the Indian horses scented her. It snorted and shook its head irritably at the odd approach by a human. Lil paused, the horse quieted and she continued.

Not yet, she silently willed the mustangs. In good time, you can make all the pandemonium you like. But not yet.

She was finally right alongside the slightly restive bunch. Gingerly, she took up the rope where it ran loosely to the rock. She reached a hand to her back, deftly drew the sharp, Bowie-style knife and began to saw.

The strands were severed in seconds. She put the rope down and began the return journey through the grass upslope. Even now, she couldn't afford to alarm the horses and have them straying and drawing attention to themselves before the time was right.

Lil regained the vantage point on the rim where she'd left the rifle. A rebellious Indian would give more for a Winchester like this than any other gun he could get. Lil took hold of it in slightly moist palms and gave up a silent prayer of thanks that Dan Kennedy had pressed it into Fanny's hands. Far better that it should be used against the Indians than by them.

She worked stealthily around the rim until the horses were between herself and the dozing Indians. She lifted the gun to her shoulder and fired three shots over the backs of the mustangs.

She worked lever and trigger as fast as she could. The near-new repeater gave her not the slightest trouble, efficiently throwing out the shells of the spent cartridges and barely warming the barrel. Judging by the shrillness of the squeals, at least one horse-hide was furrowed.

The mustangs took off, the cut rope unravelling and whipping about as they went in a thunder of hoofs and a squall of whinnies.

Chaos suddenly came down upon the sated and slumbering Indians. Startled, shouting warriors leaped up from their blankets — only to be shouldered aside and tumbled by the storming mustangs making havoc of their night-camp. A few unfortunates were trampled under hard, flashing hoofs.

Lil took pot-shots, levering and sighting, downing two Indians in quick succession. The cracks of the rifle were lost in the hideous din of yells and curses and equine shrilling.

'That's just starting to even the score,

murderers!' she cried, aware they couldn't hear her in the uproar but venting a throb of elation.

Pulses pounding, she assessed her position — and Fanny's — and decided to resist the temptation of taking out several more sitting ducks. She'd quit stirring the mêlée below while she was ahead. And while there were cartridges left in the Winchester's sixteen-shot magazine.

Given the success of the stampede, Angry-fist's bruised and confused men were unlikely to round up their half-wild mounts before daybreak. Any pursuit in the direction of Fort Dennis would then be only a distant possibility.

Covered by the confusion, Lil was able to accomplish an undetected getaway.

She made a swift return to the shed on the burned-out Kennedy spread, where Fanny awaited her, sleepless and still in a condition of blank-eyed horror.

'You must have had whatever rest you're going to get,' Lil told her. 'This place was sure pretty but it's been turned hateful. It's light enough for me. I think we should keep going till we're clear away.'

They set out to travel through the dregs of the night, taking their chances against whatever dangers it had to present.

But Lil chose an old, lesser-known route that wandered through the hills, and she kept a wary eye on their backtrail.

4

Old Trail, Old Backchat

Jackson Farraday set out from the fort as soon as the first true light had succeeded a false dawn.

Lieutenant Michael Covington had fumed impatiently, anxious to begin the search for Fanny Kennedy.

'We know where she was headed. With due respect to the colonel, tracking skills shouldn't be necessary. The woman has probably suffered some riding mishap and we'll find her along the trail.'

That didn't prove the case. Jackson's eagle-eye did, however, pick out where Fanny had met with another rider on her journey and the pair had stopped.

Covington cursed. 'Do you think this person carried her off? Maybe he was some kind of outlaw. Lord knows, we've plenty of that stripe running loose in our territory. Sheriff Hamish Howard shows little stomach for cleaning them out. The army is expected to play policeman!'

'I don't think it's anything like that,' Jackson said calmly, studying the ground and where horses had cropped at roadside grass. 'The hoofprints look familiar. Unless I miss my guess, the rider Mrs Kennedy met was Miss Lilian Goodnight, or somebody riding that grey range pony of hers.'

Covington was not pleased. 'Misfit Lil! I hope an army wife hasn't gotten involved in that brat's antics.'

Misfit Lil was Covington's *bête noir*. The girl, though a few years younger than himself, had bested him in clash after clash. The lieutenant, being handsome, dashing and always turned out impeccably, was accustomed to the admiration of the local female populace. From Lil, he didn't get it. Sparks were apt to fly when they met. She treated him like he was an inferior, as maybe he was in the outdoors skills at which she excelled. But this was a grudging admission, and he reciprocated by finding her seeming ignorance of polite manners and her familiarity with his name — she presumed to use the diminutive 'Mike' — as abominations.

'Antics?' Jackson said, raising a sun-bleached brow, but well aware of how matters stood between Covington and Lil. 'Reckon not. They stopped and spoke some, as women will. I guess, then continued their separate ways.'

Covington ordered the column to move on, too, keeping to the best trail through the broken hills for the valley occupied by Tom and Fanny Kennedy's settler kinfolks.

Long before they drew near to the place, Jackson and Colonel Lexborough's worst fears were realized.

'Looks like a trace of smoke up ahead, sir!' a sergeant called out to Covington.

Jackson let out a deep, sorrowful

sigh. He'd had his own eye on the smudge against the paleness of the early morning sky. It didn't have the look of anyone's camp-fire, nor of a breakfast fire's smoke rising fresh and orderly from a chimney.

Feeling regret and apprehension, he let Covington step up his detail's pace into a trot. Everyone thought they knew now where they'd find the missing woman; that something bad had happened at the Kennedys' ranch.

What remained of the place when they reached it sent everyone's spirits sinking. A black scar had been scorched on the green of the valley. A pair of vultures, examining the dismal scene for something they could scent but couldn't see, shambled into an awkward run and took off at the cavalry's approach.

The jumbled, blackened ruins of the Kennedys' cabin, the empty, ransacked barn and the blood-stained yard, littered with the odd broken arrow, told the bleak story. Most eloquent of all was the mound nearby of a newly dug grave, surmounted by two crosses.

A murderous raid by renegade Indians was the worst news possible. Now the whole train of events feared by Fort Dennis's commandant would be set in motion. The desk soldier, Lieutenant-General George Hamilton Morgan would be imposed upon them, full of the half-baked notions of the arrogant and inexperienced. Unforeseeable ructions would follow. Needless fatalities . . .

Jackson found names carved in haste on the very rudimentary crosses. Dan Kennedy. Edith Kennedy.

'Who buried them?' Covington demanded. 'Where's Corporal Kennedy's wife?'

Jackson was thankful that Colonel Lexborough, in his wisdom, had refused to allow the corporal to be part of the detachment. With his brother and sister-in-law dead, and the whereabouts of Fanny unknown, the man would have been beside himself.

'Maybe she had a hand in the burying,' he suggested. 'She probably left with whoever dug the graves. If you keep your men from trampling all over what's to be seen, I'll have a look around.'

Covington saw the sense in Jackson's request, and though not with the very best of grace, he passed the order that his troopers were to hold back.

The explanation soon presented itself to Jackson's sharp eyes and with a bit of supposition. The used spade and the fragments of the lumber cut for the crosses — both left in the shed — clinched it.

'I figure Fanny Kennedy might have gotten here only after it happened,' he said. (In that particular, as he later learned, he supposed wrongly.) 'Lilian Goodnight's bronc was here, too. Together, the young women buried the Kennedys and lit out not long since. During the dark, early hours anyways.

Covington frowned. 'They had no right! It would've been that raffish young follower of yours, Misfit Lil. She's interfered again, burying evidence, riding off God knows where with a vital witness — '

'Aw, do leave off, Lieutenant! Were they to let the bodies lie for the vermin? And Miss Lilian is neither raffish nor my follower. Frankly, I find her hero-worship a mite troubling.'

Misfit Lil made no secret of her ambition, unconventional for a woman, to be a scout and guide. She treated Jackson Farraday like he was some kind of idol.

Covington bit his tongue but continued to seethe. 'Where are they now then? Tell me that!'

'Probably halfway to Fort Dennis by some safer, lesser-ridden trail that's unlikely to be watched by Angry-fist and his hellions. Maybe I can catch us up with them.'

Covington figured it would be ignominious if his patrol was to return empty-handed to the fort after it had been reached and alerted by two women, one of whom the detachment had been sent out to find.

'I'd be obliged if you'd do that, Mr Farraday.'

His report on the scene of the destruction and slayings would have to rely on cursory rather than detailed examination. The main facts were clear enough.

The troopers lined out again the way they'd come till Jackson led them on to a branch trail. The minor route hadn't been regularly travelled in an age. Weeds grew across their path. At one place a slip had obliterated a fifty-yard stretch. A deadfall blocking the trail had been partly dragged to one side. Inches of humus were revealed and it was riddled with ant colonies underneath, as yet undiscovered by winged or other predators.

Each step gave Jackson the evidence to back his hunch. Weed stems had been recently broken and crushed by hoofs. Slip rubble had been rolled, showing rocks' damp sides not yet baked dry by the sun. The deadfall hadn't shifted by itself.

Covington grumbled.

'The Goodnight girl must be crazy, risking necks on a dangerous trail like this by night. Like as not we'll find they've ridden clear off some bend and plunged to their deaths!'

'If you recollect there was a half-moon,' Jackson said. 'That would be more than enough for Lil Goodnight. She knows this neck of the woods inside out, as I'm sure you also recall. If she thought they'd come to grief, she would've given up and camped on the trail, till first light anyway. She's a very resourceful young lady.'

Covington didn't like to be reminded of it. After that, he said no more, but Jackson was sure he continued his grumbling silently.

They caught up with Lil and Fanny some miles short of the fort. To Jackson, Covington's relief was pal-pable. Himself, he was too deeply worried about the implications of the

Indian raid for the garrison and the Silver Vein country to be concerned about the detail of overtaking them.

'Halt!' Covington bawled after the two riders. He rode hard up to them and drew rein in a shower of dust.

'Huh!' Lil snorted scornfully to her companion. 'It's God's gift to the cavalry, Mike Covington. Too late to do any good, as always. Don't let him bully you, Fanny!'

'I heard that, Miss Goodnight!' Covington snapped, his face reddening. 'I'd trouble you to curb your uncivil tongue. Mrs Kennedy will be escorted to the fort in my care. You've meddled far enough.'

'Meddled?' Lil asked, her grey eyes smouldering, disbelieving. 'What the hell do you mean by that?'

'Hey! Settle down, you two,' Jackson said, uncomfortable.

They ignored him.

Stiff-backed, Covington said, 'You did wrong, interring the bodies of Dan and Edith Kennedy.'

Lil tossed her head. 'Horsefeathers! Which of your precious army regulations says you leave the victims of massacres for coyotes and suchlike? Even a fool like you must know that ain't civilized, Mike Covington.'

The lieutenant bristled, unsure how he should react to the dressing-down in front of his men by this blunt-mouthed, eccentric girl.

'I've got a job to do, Miss Goodnight,' he said, gulping down his rage, 'and part of that job is furnishing proof. The bodies should have been taken in, officially and legally identified and so forth. Cause of death determined. The authorities won't take kindly to your intervention.'

Lil sat her calm grey horse and folded her arms.

'Really? Well, I don't much give a damn whether they take kindly to it or not, it's what Fanny and I decided was right. We didn't have horses to haul bodies, less we used our own mounts, leading 'em in on foot. That didn't make a lick of sense.'

Jackson had heard Lil give Covington backchat on numerous occasions. He leaned across, tugged at Covington's sleeve, and received an irritable glare.

'What is it, man?'

'We've still a piece to ride and these ladies will have had a harrowing time,' Jackson reminded, thinking mostly of the corporal's wife and the husband himself anxiously waiting for word at the fort.

Covington huffed, getting a cinch on his temper.

'You're right. Angry-fist has gone on the rampage again. Reports have to be made urgently. But cattleman Goodnight's wayward daughter is such a little pest . . . ' Before Lil could protest, he signalled for the column to proceed. '*Forward*!'

Jackson privately reflected it was a sad situation. He and Michael Covington had both had occasion to be thankful for Misfit Lil's interventions; had known times when she'd proved more of an asset than a liability. Her logic was generally incontestable.

And 'little'? Why, Lil reached to his shoulder. He was tall for a man and, while she wasn't an Amazon, that still meant she was tall for a girl. She had a certain appealingly youthful beauty. She didn't lack for brains and initiative, and she could handle a gun better than most any professional shootist he'd met.

Miss Lilian was right, Jackson thought — Mike Covington was a fool: a fool not to appreciate she had all the qualities from which he might benefit as a professional soldier posted in the West. Of close ages, they should have made a match. She could show the West Point graduate a thing or two if he'd let her. The pity was, his pride wouldn't let him. And Lil was too damn much of a rebel ever to honour and obey the man, let alone absorb some of the Eastern respect for fine manners he might teach her.

Instead, she'd picked himself, Jackson Farraday, as an object worthy of her affections. Which was absurd. If it was destiny, then they wouldn't have been born so many years apart. He was about double her age. Lil tempted him, and men in this place and time did hitch up with younger females, but he knew a relationship could end only in hurt. She wasn't for him. The years would likely sap him of his vitality while Misfit Lil was still in her raging prime.

But his personal problems were for the moment all grossly overshadowed by the unwelcome development in the matter of the reservation jumpers.

Jackson swore quietly. Again, the defectors had turned their red hands to murder. Once Fanny Kennedy's and Lil Goodnight's stories were out, it would be impossible to control the issue at a local level. Fort Dennis was going to be in more trouble than it could shake a stick at. Old and petty squabbles between Covington and Lil, and the girl's impractical preferences, would be immaterial.

They rode out of the broken hills and

through a last screening line of timber. The fort hove into sight on the flats, a vague outline dancing in the heat haze drawn out of the ground by the mid-morning sun. From Colonel Brook Lexborough down, lives and careers there were about to be turned topsy-turvy by the agitators in Washington. Nothing would stop it now.

The glory-seeking General Morgan would have his day.

5

Feeling the Heat

A strange feeling of unreality hung over the parade ground at Fort Dennis. A breeze lifted dust in intermittent flurries but did little to relieve for the waiting, silent company the rigours of the sweat-raising, blue-collar-dampening heat. Colours fluttered feebly.

Only the handful of men manning the stockade's catwalks on lookout duty were escaping the worst of the ordeal. Otherwise, the entire garrison, with the exception of a small squad despatched for an escort, was assembled on the parade ground. Infantry, cavalry, band and colour guard were drawn up in wilting lines of discomfort.

Jackson Farraday had bothered to attend the arrival of Lieutenant-General George Hamilton Morgan from Washington simply because he was of a mind to stand four-square with his military friends and companions of several years; lend them the moral support of his presence.

But as the minutes dragged on, past the time designated for the general's appearance, he grew as weary as the soldiers lined up for the occasion in full uniform and kept baking in the sun as per received orders from the War Department top brass.

It seemed injury might soon be added to insult. A private went chalk-white, buckled at the knees and fainted in a rifle-clattering heap.

As a civilian, and therefore to considerable extent his own master, Jackson never felt easy on occasions of ceremonial inspection. It was a side of army life for which he had little stomach. In this respect, he reflected, his thoughts ran along similar lines to young Miss Lilian Goodnight's, though unlike her he would never be so free with his tongue in their expression. But

Lil, of course, had no invitation here today, and he'd no business to be letting her invade his thoughts.

Finally, nigh on an hour late, the squad sent to the railyards at Green River to meet and accompany General Morgan and his aide to the fort was sighted.

From the tower above the main gate, a voice cried, 'Detachment coming, sir. Two officers with the escort . . . and a buckboard, sir!' The last information was imparted with an edge of surprise.

'Thank you, Corporal,' Colonel Brook Lexborough said. 'Sergeant O'Reilly, put the company at attention.'

Jackson was standing behind the colonel on a specially erected dais. While the iron-lunged sergeant bawled his orders, he murmured, 'Buckboard? Why should they need one of those?'

The gates swung open and the escort and the fort's significant guests rode in. There was indeed a buckboard, groaning under a heavy load of several crates covered with a canvas. Green River was largely a railroad town, run by the Denver & Rio Grande Western Railway, but Jackson recognized the green-painted buckboard and the pair of sturdy harness horses that drew it. The combination was one of three for hire at a Green River livery stable. He conjectured that its procurement and loading might explain the visitors' delayed arrival.

Brassy notes issued from the band, flags were jerked smartly to a vertical position and senior officers snapped salutes.

General Morgan reminded Jackson of a picture of the late French emperor Napoleon Bonaparte. He was of sturdy build, had a florid complexion and his eyes were small, dark and pig-like. He returned the salutes with a gloved hand raised to his hatbrim. The casualness of the gesture struck Jackson as false, contrived.

He leaned across the pommel of his saddle and cast an intent eye over the troops drawn up for his inspection. He sniffed dismissively, suggestive of a man detecting an offensive smell.

Colonel Lexborough descended from the dais and strode forward to stand at attention near the general's horse. The heat-fatigued band petered to a ragged stop.

'Colonel Brook Lexborough, sir, commanding officer, Fort Dennis. On behalf of the men of my command, I welcome you.'

Morgan sniffed again. He looked around him, as though taking in regrettable sights. Only when he'd seen enough to make him frown did he reply, 'At ease, Colonel. And put your troops at parade rest.'

'Would you care to address the men, sir?'

'I would, Colonel.'

Morgan dismounted awkwardly and walked stiffly to the dais, followed by his adjutant. He removed his hat to wipe his brow. His hair was damp and thinning on top. The patch of scalp showing was an angry red.

'When I got something to say, I have it out straight.' He indicated his aide. 'Major Ezra Creede and I intended to make changes hereabouts. I see now they're sorely needed. We don't have the time at this moment, nor is it appropriate, for us to explain. The Fort Dennis record is not good. Its results are unacceptable and, by God, that will be changed! But I will say I observe too many soldiers here today whose turnout is a disgrace — missing buttons and scuffed boots, rifle stocks scratched and plainly abused . . . and so on. Major Creede will implement an immediate programme of rectification through your officers.'

Major Creede, tall and brooding with a hint of severity in his sharp features, nodded approvingly. Cynical amusement put a crooked grin on his thin lips.

Colonel Lexborough lowered his head and examined his boot toes, tactfully hiding his reactions from all. To comment would be unthinkable insubordination.

Jackson's opinion of General Morgan and the War Department's new strategy to solve the Angry-fist problem sank to rock bottom. The general's first words had confirmed he was a fool.

In reality, the frontier forts were too far apart and their garrisons too small for optimum results. With average strengths of less than a hundred men each, it was often difficult even to patrol sprawling territories adequately. Tracking Indians deemed hostile by the government was difficult enough. The soldiers were bewildered by their enemies' mobility, knowledge of the terrain, and tactical sagacity. Reduced to weariness by the rings run around them, the troops were then further stressed by the monotony of parade-ground drills, tedious routine guard duty, and fatigue duty.

The money wasn't provided for replacement of uniforms and equipment, and only the fanatical few, like Michael Covington determined to preserve the gloss of his West Point image, found the motivation necessary to maintain worn outfits in peak condition.

All this was understood by the reasonable Colonel Lexborough and the men like Jackson who worked from time to time alongside the military.

Having delivered his cruelly critical verdict. Morgan stumped down the steps from the dais followed by Creede who took a discreet, measured swallow from a rum flask.

'Stomach ulcers,' he said, by way of explanation to the colonel who was alongside him. 'Medicinal.' He stowed the flask and tapped his hip. 'Has to accompany me everywhere.'

The fiery liquor hit his drawn, hard-looking belly and he belched.

Jackson made a mental note that at the earliest occasion he would personally give the major more discomfort by acquainting him with the uninformed absurdity of the general's censure. He would take him to task for it, even if only in mild argument. If the chance arose, he would speak his mind to the general himself.

★ ★ ★

Over the following days, the newcomers proved themselves every bit as disagreeable as their arrival had suggested. They instigated endless drills and kit inspections, delivered text-book lectures on military tactics and laid blame on all and sundry, bar Washington, for the failure to apprehend the elusive recalcitrant, Angry-fist.

The secret contained in the heavy crates on the buckboard leaked out and was spread to the gossiping township of Silver Vein. Jackson suspected the general, through Major Creede, saw to it that this was done deliberately, possibly to enhance the civilians' feelings of security and give Morgan stature in the community which could ultimately be fed back to impress the Eastern newspapers.

Misfit Lil sought out Jackson in

76

McHendry's saloon.

'What's this secret weapon — this Gatling gun?' she asked.

'It's a hand-crank-operated gun with ten barrels that rotate around a central shaft. When assembled, it don't look much, mounted on a carriage that's scarce more than an axle on a couple of wagon wheels, but it can fire one thousand two hundred rounds per minute.'

Lil's jaw dropped, but her moment of hesitation was brief. 'There must be a snag,' she said.

'Several. It weighs nothing less than ninety pounds, so it isn't especially manoeuvrable in the field — leastways, no field around this neck of the woods — and it needs up to four operators. The newest model accepts two rows of .45/.70 cartridges. While one row is being fed into the gun, the other can be reloaded, which allows sustained fire, they say. But it's also prone to jamming and although it's been around since the War Between the States, many artillery-men have little time for it.'

Lil sensed that Jackson wasn't impressed, so it followed she wasn't either.

'Hmm! If these Eastern dudes have got any savvy at all, they should know dragging around a cumbersome secret weapon won't work against fast-moving Injuns in the canyonlands. Anyhow, that blowhard Sheriff Howard has been singing General Morgan's praises, which means they have to be all wrong.'

Silver Vein's peace officer, Hamish Howard, was an incompetent who largely spent his time collecting taxes — a perk of his office — and buttering-up influential, voters. He'd frequently left matters of civilian law enforcement for Fort Dennis to clean up, earning its exasperation.

Rustlers, bank robbers, horse thieves, gunrunners, peddlers to Indians of whiskey . . . scum of such stripe had run free in places where Howard had jurisdiction till the army was forced to step in, aided by Jackson Farraday and Misfit Lil.

Howard was not displeased to see

the tables turned and heat being put on Colonel Lexborough and his company.

Changing the subject slightly, Lil said, 'I'd like to see these desk-soldier chuckleheads. What's this pre-campaign ball everybody 'cept me's being invited to?'

Jackson's laugh was brittle. 'Nothing more than an opportunity for General George Hamilton Morgan to pursue his political agenda. He cuts a dash in society and I guess he likes to see reports of himself on the pages of newspapers where such occasions are covered.'

'You're going, aren't you?' Lil said forthrightly. 'Will you let me be your partner?'

Jackson laughed again. 'A ball in a mess hall is hardly Misfit Lil's scene, is it?'

'Oh, I can dress up like a lady if I've a mind to. 'Sides, like I said, I'd admire to see these idiots who reckon they can catch Angry-fist when we can't.'

Jackson hesitated. Then he said warily, 'All right then. Mrs Lexborough is compiling the official guest list. I'll try to fix that your name goes on.'

He knew that Lil approved of the colonel's wife. In fact, few people could find an uncomplimentary word for Mrs Geraldine Lexborough. In her late thirties and despite postings to some rugged parts of the frontier, she maintained an elegance and charm everyone envied. She worked hard at the fort, paying special attention to the welfare and needs of the wives of the enlisted men and seeing that some comforts were provided in their spartan quarters. Although Mrs Lexborough would never stoop to behave like Lilian Goodnight, or condone her outrageous exploits, she had a sympathy for the Flying G rancher's rascal daughter.

And Lil had a soft spot for 'Gerry', but Jackson didn't know how this would be resolved into appreciation of a grand social occasion of the kind Lil would normally avoid.

He shrugged. 'Knowing your tastes, you'll probably be bored rigid, but I'm sure it can't do any harm.'

It was a comment and a mistake he was to remember and regret.

6

The Unwelcome Gift

Everybody who was anybody for miles around had been invited to the ball at Fort Dennis in honour of Lieutenant-General George Hamilton Morgan. The officers' mess hall had been cleared, hastily repainted and decked out with bunting. Its wooden floor was waxed to shining perfection for the dancing.

A stream of buggies and carriages of all kinds brought the guests from the township, the men rigged out in their Sunday-best clothes and the women in a colourful variety of frilly frocks. When Lilian Goodnight rode up to the main gates on her range horse and dressed in her usual men's duds, several onlookers giggled and the sergeant on duty tried to refuse her entrance.

'I'm going to the fandango escorted

by Mr Farraday,' she protested. She slapped a large carpetbag tied on behind the cantle of her saddle. 'My ball gown's in here. Let me over to the stables. I can change in a spare stall.'

With a show of reluctance, but something of a grin, the sergeant let her have her way. Frankly, he'd already had enough of the nonsense dished out by the men from Washington and he didn't greatly care if the girl wanted to make a mockery of herself or the fine occasion. It was all a damn foofaraw anyways.

Inside the stables, it was gloomy and reeked of hay, ammonia, horsesweat and dung. The soldier in charge was openly friendlier than the men at the gates. He appreciated good, well-kept broncs and told her he would grain and groom Rebel and let her use the tack room to change.

When she emerged, he was stunned. So, too, was Jackson Farraday when she came up to him where he was waiting for her outside the mess hall.

'I didn't recognize you,' he lied,

though it might almost have been the truth.

Lilian Goodnight was radiantly beautiful in a new and becoming purple gown. Her dark hair had been brushed till it shone under the soft lights and her eyes sparkled with interest and a keen appreciation of the celebratory scene. It proved she could surely be a beauty if she took time to tidy herself up and apply a little face powder and lip rouge — feminine fripperies for which she said often enough she had no time.

More, the makeover had accentuated somehow the fundamentals of her genuine, natural charm. She was tall and slim, while the tan which tinted her flawless skin was a sure sign of the health in her well-formed, youthful body.

The hall was packed and abuzz with conversation. Musicians were tuning fiddles. As always in frontier communities, the men outnumbered the women, but there were about forty army wives, ranchers' wives and daughters and townswomen, including the famously pretty girls who staffed Ma Coutts's Traveller's Hotel where Lil herself had once found employment and a refuge during a memorable, bleak winter.

Jackson thought none of the girls more eye-pleasing than Lil in her unaccustomed outfit. She had done him proud and he wasn't ashamed to have her on his arm. You never knew with Misfit Lil; she was unpredictable and unreadable — always seemed to be one jump ahead.

Sheriff Howard glowered some, as though Lil had pulled the stunt of her transformation at his particular expense. Being left alone to collect tax money and enjoy a safe and lazy time ruled Sheriff Howard's life. Lilian Goodnight was trouble and he wished she wasn't here. Likely she was fixing to upset this new apple cart which was transferring the voters' attentions to the failings of Colonel Brook Lexborough and his command.

But he had to admit that right now

she was plumb bewitching. Even normally, in her men's duds, she inspired his lustful dreams. He wasn't the only one in Silver Vein who'd put his mind to work on how to create a situation in which she'd be obliged to make his fantasies reality.

He didn't expect the impossible. Just the once — but a thorough encounter — would do to satisfy his curiosity and give him something to recall for stimulation. Maybe if he could jail her on some pretext, which shouldn't be hard given her wild ways, she might be conveniently beholden to him . . . But no — his predecessor had tried that and found Lil gave no favours, nor accepted them.

The Reverend Titus Fisher said, 'Tell me, Sheriff, is that dreadful young woman also to be presented to our distinguished visitors?'

Silver Vein's sniffy, full-bearded sky-pilot was another who disapproved of Ben Goodnight's child even before being properly horrified by the whispers of immoral conduct in Boston — the salacious detail of which, however, he'd sought out with alacrity.

Howard grunted. 'Seems like, Reverend.'

'Well I never!' the preacher said. It was a stock phrase for him — the one he used universally to express scandal, censure or whatever response was demanded but lay beyond his imagination to produce.

Fanny Kennedy was among the few women not caught up in the twittering excitement any social occasion brought to predominantly dull lives.

'Why so glum, Fanny?' Lil asked while her husband was out of earshot.

'Tom is in a foul mood,' she faltered. 'His comrades are finding the men from Washington a burden. They reckon their imposition here has something to do with the foolishness of Tom's kinfolk in claiming an isolated and dangerous section. Tom is made a butt of their resentment.'

Reading between the lines, it wasn't

hard to work out this had led to fruitless argument between Thomas and Fanny. Fort life put a strain on marital relationships at the best of times. Accommodation in married men's quarters was primitive, despite the best efforts of those like Mrs Geraldine Lexborough who sought to improve it and ameliorate the deprivations.

Before the recent events, scuttlebutt had suggested little love was lost between the Kennedys, but they were Catholics and any thought of divorce, though always impractical in a hard setting, was doubly horrifying.

'It makes me furious,' Lil complained to Jackson when Fanny had gone to rejoin her husband. 'What the Kennedys had wasn't very romantic and all, but these popinjays from Washington with their spit-and-polish notions have more to answer for than they can know. They're ten times worse than Mike Covington!'

Jackson's heart, though lifted by Lil's success in sprucing herself up for the occasion, was heavy, too, for any number of reasons. His mood wasn't improved when General Morgan and Major Creede arrived to applause from the assembly and a lively bar or two of 'The Star-spangled Banner' from the musicians.

Gerry Lexborough stepped forward, as hostess, to welcome the officers assigned to remedy the shortcomings of her husband's command. She was a totally, naturally gracious woman who always deported herself like a lady. She was also maturely beautiful, with glowing, ivory skin and auburn hair threaded lightly with grey. Her figure was full and generously bosomed, but had the firmness of a woman ten years younger. She wore a dark-green, flowing dress of some hard, shiny material that made her movements delightful.

General Morgan preened himself and behaved like he was in an Eastern seaboard drawing-room.

'Ah! The colonel's absolutely charming wife. My adjutant, Major Creede, and I didn't expect the chance to — uh

— have the company here of such a beautiful lady.'

Mrs Lexborough extended a hand.

'Everyone here, of course, has heard about you, General,' she said, which was tactfully noncommittal.

He bent over her hand. 'Your charm has not been exaggerated, ma'am.'

She curtsied. 'Thank you, sir.'

Morgan gave her a smarmy smile. 'Eastern manners are missed out here in the Wild West by the man of the world, the man of fine manners.'

Watching from the ring of spectators, Lil growled under her breath to Jackson. 'God, these Eastern folks are hard to stomach!'

Morgan turned to Major Creede, an attentive two paces to the rear. 'Let me have my gift for our hostess.'

Creede handed him a brightly wrapped package which he in turn presented to Mrs Lexborough.

'Why,' she said, momentarily taken aback, 'this is a surprise. I've done nothing to deserve — '

'My good lady,' the general inter-posed firmly but with a leer, 'you will prove a most *obliging* hostess, I'm sure. Now do open the wrappings and let everyone see.'

The colonel gave Gerry a prompting nod and she peeled off coloured paper to reveal a slender, gold-hilted stiletto in a crimson sheath of soft velvet.

'Why . . . ' she murmured, uncertain quite how she should react. 'It's — beautiful. Thank you.'

'Italian,' the general said. 'A pure work of art that embodies the simple elegance of the early Renaissance. Medici, you know.'

A ripple of awe ran through the onlookers. 'Well I never!' the Reverend Fisher said.

The dagger was about nine inches long. The hilt was moulded in the form of a slender, naked girl standing feet and legs tightly together and with arms lifted and hands clasped above her golden head. Swelling golden breasts were tipped with garnets, glinting red against the gold.

Gerry drew it from the sheath. The blade was slim and triangular. It looked completely deadly efficient. A single thrust of the little toy into heart or lung, bunched spinal nerves or brain, would kill the strongest man. She suppressed a shudder that was noted by the more observant, put it back swiftly in the sheath and turned it over awkwardly in her hands.

Ezra Creede leaned his head forward. 'Will make a fine letter opener or paper knife, ma'am. And a very valuable antique to boot.'

'Hundreds of years old,' Morgan emphasized quietly. 'I'm sure you'll want to show your gratitude later.'

Then, over the hubbub of the impressed gathering, Misfit Lil said stridently, 'Huh! It's a shivery gewgaw, whatever price you put on it. Who cares for hundred-year-old Italian trash? Out in the canyon-lands, I could show you buried caches of Injun arrowheads that are *really* ancient.'

Creede wheeled, seeking out the speaker in the press of what he'd liked to think were admirers. He fixed her with a steely eye.

'Who is that ignorant woman? Has she no manners or taste?'

''Course she don't,' someone piped up. 'That's Misfit Lil!'

'Does she work your town's saloons?'

'No, I don't!' Lil said indignantly.

The Reverend Fisher pushed forward with a cough.

'Howsomever, she hasn't prized her virtue. Silver Vein apologizes, sir. Miss Goodnight is a rancher's disowned brat of a daughter.'

Sheriff Howard chimed in, 'She's got a smart mouth, Major. Gets above herself.'

Fisher added sententiously, 'A wilful girl comes to no good end, and the Good Book says so.'

'Ain't hard to know who your friends are around here!' Lil snapped.

Meanwhile, Gerry surreptitiously hid the sinister dagger away in her reticule.

It *was* beautiful, but she didn't like it and thought it a poor choice for a gift. Too expensive. Too coldly evil in the purpose of its design which was surely assassination.

Colonel Lexborough, a man who knew how to nip a developing crisis in the bud if he had the chance, gave a signal for the dance band to begin playing.

Ma Coutts's girls, whose social accomplishments were comprehensive and who were allowed by their employer to attend their township's Saturday-night dances, took their partners and, led by the colonel and his lady, opened the ball according to Mrs Lexborough's careful prior arrangements.

The dancers performed a grand march, or polonaise, a solemn processional in three-four time. Lines of couples wove their graceful way across the waxed floor of the improvised ballroom in intricate patterns.

But this was not what General Morgan wanted. Sniffily, he conferred with Major Creede who carried instructions to the musicians at the first pause.

The biggest revolution of the century in social dancing was the growing popularity of the waltz, danced in triple time. But in fashionable circles in the East, such as Morgan moved in, the latest version was the Boston waltz, of a slower tempo than the popular Viennese dance.

This was the dance Morgan now demanded, and he chose Gerry Lexborough for his partner.

'I knew it!' Lil hissed to Jackson. 'The lecherous old bastard couldn't wait to get his hands on her.'

The waltz incorporated a close hold and constant turning clockwise while the partners travelled counter-clockwise around the room. The giddying movement could rob a woman of her senses and produce a feeling of euphoria. Though broad-minded, Lil could understand right now why waltzes were condemned on moral grounds.

With this pair as partners, it *did*

appear vulgar and sinful.

Jackson agreed. 'Yeah, it looks kind of wicked for the obnoxious general to have seized on the colonel's good woman. A Virginia Reel would've been more fitting.'

The elegant and gracious Mrs Lexborough, known for her modest reserve, was being subjected to participation in a coarse display. As they executed long, gliding steps to the rhythm supplied by scraping fiddles and tuneful piano, Morgan slipped his right hand lower and lower on his partner's anatomy. Lil was convinced the boorish brute's sausage-like fingers were kneading the flesh under the satiny green gown. Gerry, of course, could do nothing about it and had to suffer the indignity silently.

Lil resolved that she hadn't finished speaking her mind.

She also took the opportunity, when Lieutenant Michael Covington came to speak with Jackson by the refreshment tables, to register protest with him.

'Your general should be horse-whipped, Mike, forcing himself on poor Mrs Lexborough. His waltzing is obscene.'

Covington coloured. 'I don't know what you mean, Miss Goodnight. Respectable society embraces the waltz. It's accepted even at the English court. I understand Queen Victoria is a keen and expert ballroom dancer with a special love of the waltz.'

'But there is a proper and a vulgar manner of holding a partner! Being pawed by an animal isn't made right because it's done to music.'

'Well . . . ' Covington said, flustered, 'you'd be a fine one to object on any grounds of what's the correct etiquette!'

He quickly slipped away into a crowd of guests to escape an unseemly confrontation. Jackson restrained Lil from following.

'There's nothing he or any of the soldiery can do. The general and his adjutant have rank over everybody. They call the shots, I guess.'

'Thank God there're no career consequences for me!' Lil said. 'The minute I get half a chance, I'm going to have it out with these snakes from Washington.'

'Do you think that'll be wise?' Jackson asked. 'Aren't you being a mite headstrong?'

But Misfit Lil, fuming, wasn't listening. She didn't conceive then of consequences for herself that she'd find just as unpleasant as any her Fort Dennis friends might suffer.

7

Hard Hand of Discipline

Lil's dismay and anger only deepened as the evening wore on. She began to wonder whether it had been worth the effort to secure her invitation to the ball, though she sipped her drink appreciatively.

Liquor flowed freely. It was no cheap redeye, but bonded stuff supplied, it was said, at the general's personal expense.

'Smooth as molasses. The general knows what to drink but little else, I reckon. This sure is tasting liquor and not the kind for gulping.'

Though Lil herself was wont to drink nothing but the best imported whiskey in McHendry's saloon in Silver Vein, the quality booze did nothing to brighten her mood, or make the conduct and humour of others more pleasing to her eyes.

Fanny Kennedy, unused to strong drink, argued with husband Tom and they went to different parts of the room, as though to sulk.

Lil couldn't find the motivation to tease Mike Covington, a game from which she ordinarily derived considerable amusement.

She and Jackson overheard, though clearly no one was meant to, a disturbing exchange between Major Ezra Creede and Colonel Lexborough.

'Your wife is a fine figure of a woman, Colonel,' the major murmured in his ear. 'I see the general is tolerably taken. I'm sure it would enhance your career prospects if you were to allow him to share some moments with her privately. Later, when we go to your quarters, it might be convenient if we both disappeared to mine on some plausible pretext or other and left the general and Mrs Lexborough to get on with — er — transactions. It's how these things are done in polite society in Washington.'

Lil felt her insides squirm at the blatancy of the proposition. Gerry Lexborough wouldn't be the least bit interested in receiving the desk general's attentions. She was no saloon floosie!

Lexborough, using his wits, pretended to be too dumb to understand the full implications. He turned down the major's suggestion as though the fault would be on his and his wife's part.

'Oh, my wife and I will not be seeking such — um — advantages. We take and give no favours.'

Creede said cuttingly, and not without a note of warning, 'Well, of course, some men have no ambition, but the general is headed for the highest offices in the land. Once the elimination of Angryfist has enhanced his active-combat record, there'll be no stopping him.'

Jackson, aware Lil's ears were flapping, dragged her away from the alcove where they'd almost stumbled in on the pair.

'That was disgusting,' Lil said.

'It was a private conversation, not for your young hearing.'

'Nor anyone else's, I should think!'

Later, during a lull in the revels, General Morgan held forth on his theories on dealing with rebellious Indians. An audience of impressionable officers, Covington among them, hung on his words.

'We have to reassert our authority over these savages. The depredations of Angry-fist should not have been allowed to escalate. I shall have action from you, or know the reason why not! Attempts to pacify the hostiles have failed. We must intimidate them.'

Lil, who'd roamed away from Jackson, frustrated by his quiet forbearance in the face of so much provocation, said loudly, 'Would that it were so simple!'

The general was complexioned with a tendency to turn purple. His face darkened.

'Who said that?'

'I did,' Lil admitted, pushing her way forward through the press of army men. 'The problem isn't some bureaucratic abstraction, you know. If you're set on all-out war, it'll need the time and energy of men who know the people and the land to develop suitable tactics and strategy. Men like my friend Jackson Farraday.'

'Hogwash!' the general blurted, fixing on her with his small, pig-like eyes. 'A mere gal and her friends can't tell the army what needs to be done. It's absurd!'

Lil raised her shoulders, delightful in the becoming ball gown, in a shrug.

'Ask Mr Farraday then. He's one of your educated men; speaks seven languages and God knows how many Indian lingoes. He'll tell you how successful officers on the frontier develop their methods through personal observation, by trial and error, by word of mouth, or by individual ingenuity. Fool policies made up by idiots sitting on their fat asses in cushioned chairs

103

back East count for nothing here.'

Her little speech left Morgan about breathing fire.

'Missy, it's a mere fleeting bother you have in your Silver Vein country! These men you see before you will be trained to use my Gatling gun. It'll be turned on your Angry-fist and he and his men will be blown away like chaff on the wind!'

Lil nodded. 'Oh, yes — the Gatling. Why the hell have you brought such a useless weapon for the terrain and the job at hand? Man, you sure don't know much about Indian fighting. You'd do better to teach your soldiers how to shoot the pip out of an ace of spades at fifty yards with a hand-gun!'

'I suppose you'll tell me you can do that,' Morgan spluttered.

'Why, yeah. I can at that. They call me Princess of Pistoleers hereabouts, and I surely outshot your army contestant at our last shooting match.'

Sheriff Howard, who'd been deter-mined to help General Morgan reap the full publicity benefits of his mission, bulled forward, huffing.

'Shuddup, Misfit Lil! Yuh might think yuh're smart, but yuh're a disgrace to a decent community.'

The Reverend Titus Fisher backed him up. 'She sure is. Everything a young female shouldn't be — tough, lippy and a known loose character. A harlot.'

'That's a damn lie, and you a preacher!' Lil retorted. 'I've only ever made love to a man by choice. Fact is, I've far better morals than a general who paws his dancing partner's backside!'

Morgan's face congested with apoplectic anger. The fury in his voice made his big florid cheeks tremble.

'You sassy little bitch!' he roared.

'This ain't Washington, General. We don't cotton to underhandedness and bigots. What counts is what a man is, what he does. No favours, no fears.'

She realized she'd been drawn into razzing the general something fierce.

Maybe she'd let her quick, sharp tongue run away with her. Only now did she notice out of the corner of her eye that the hatchet-faced aide, Major Ezra Creede, was standing close behind her. She saw Morgan deliver an unspoken but understood order with a nod of his head and an imperious motion of his hand.

Creede reached out for her at the same moment she made to beat a retreat.

'No, you don't, mouthy brat! You're getting your comeuppance!'

With his left hand, he grabbed her left wrist in a sudden iron grip and pulled it up firmly behind her in an armlock. Setting himself down on a seat pushed forward by an astute sergeant, who'd gleaned a notion of what he had in mind, he pulled and pushed her over his knees. In terms of unarmed combat, it was very expertly done. She was powerless to stop him without breaking her arm.

Her head plunged and her ass was

elevated. Creede promptly turned up the skirts of ball gown and petticoat to her shoulders, revealing silk stockings, garters and elegant dancing shoes.

'There's only one way to deal with a shrew like you. That's a damn good spanking!'

Verdict and sentence met with guffaws and popular acclaim from a crowd well liquored up. Women joined in the laughter, some coarsely, some nervously. Lil had no chance of reprieve or escape. Her last, but minimal, protection was the thin cotton drawers stretched over the firm rounds of her bottom.

'You can't do this!' she cried.

'But I can and I will.'

'Ain't she got nice — hips?' said a voice, audibly drooling over the sight.

Another whooped. 'Sure is a purty thing, fellers!'

'Unhitch them d-drawers!' a soldier urged with a drunken hiccup. 'Slip 'em down to her kn-knees an' do it on the raw!'

God, he wouldn't, would he . . . ?

Hot damn, yes! The swine was fixing to go along with the rabble.

'I think I might,' Creede said in oily agreement. His intrusive fingers groped under her waist and upturned clothes for the ends of the drawstrings.

'*No* — !' she protested.

It was the ultimate indignity. With two efficient tugs, and to a chorus of unkind cheers, Creede lowered the body of her underwear to a band of crumples, exposing the cheeks of her buttocks to sudden chill and more. The fascinated of both sexes crowded round to view the spectacle. The eyes on her were palpable.

'Misfit Lil's time has come,' Sheriff Howard said, hot-necked and thick-voiced. 'An' it's fittin'. She's allus bin a li'le slut.'

The unfair humiliation of it was more than Lil could take. The baring of a woman's bottom in public was a remarkable event that would be talked about around Silver Vein for weeks. She'd never been ashamed of her body, despite living in an age that professed nether regions and all their functions to be degrading to the human whole. But upended like she was, those close behind her must be seeing way more than anyone should.

Details surely wouldn't escape the avid curiosity of the advantageously placed. She wasn't a newborn babe or a child. Her lower belly with its diamond patch of black curls was held tight against Creede's leg, but awareness of the gawkers excited an involuntary, paradoxical reaction. She felt an incipient dampness. Moisture — it purely had to be from fear — must be darkening a visible edging of hair. And to her frantic mind, it felt that recesses put illegitimately on view had filled out and separated.

Highly amused, Creede said to his audience, 'Satisfied? You see before you a sweet and tempting ass crying out for correction. Beginning now!'

Though he spared Lil prolonged inspection, he didn't spare her the full force of his hard hand. She jerked as the first sharp smack fell.

'Ouch! That hurt, you pervert!'

'The object is it should,' Creede reminded. 'We're teaching you a lesson.'

Morgan snarled, 'Get on with it, Major! Give the upstart trollop the damn' good larruping she's asked for!'

Creede began to lay a pattern of ringing, rhythmic slaps all over Lil's quivering backside with obvious relish.

Her legs kicked wide, restricted only by the stretched ring of the concertinaed drawers at her knees. The dancing shoes were flung off her feet.

'S-stop it!' she blurted. 'Let me up!'

But though she struggled, as any strong person would simply in reflex, Creede kept her doubled over.

'Discipline, girly!' Then, venom in his voice. 'I want you to feel every hit . . . every bit of shame!'

With his hold on her arm, he thrust her head and shoulders well down. She was thus kept in an attitude of forced submission over his hard knees, unclothed buttocks stuck up in the air flaunted along with whatever else was incidentally exhibited by her flurry of wriggles and squirming and the subtly progressive, thigh-opening insinuation of a leg between hers.

Damn it! She didn't deserve this embarrassment. She clenched her teeth and lips, suppressing gasps of pain.

Few among the supposedly polite company made any attempt to avert their astonished gaze from what was extremely improper by the standards of the day. Creede's brisk hand rose and fell.

Miss Purity Wadsworth, president of the Silver Vein Ladies' Temperance Society said approvingly, 'That's it — beat the tar out of her! Miss Goodnight's a constant scandal. Her pa should've given her a hiding thisaway long back, when she was a disrespectful button.'

'Nope,' a man said. 'Reckon it's more int'restin' now she's fully grow'd. Ain't it a plumb naughty picture — white knickers brung down into jest a loop an' the cheeks warmed pink?'

Though in middle age, he'd never viewed a post-adolescent female pitched at so revealing an angle, not even in lewd prints touted surreptitiously in saloons.

Refinement and sensibility were out the door; prurience was in. Licking his lips, the mealy-mouthed Titus Fisher quoted scripture in supposed justification of the public chastisement.

'She's been a trial to her parent and an insult to general morality way too long . . . 'For if we sin wilfully after that we have received the knowledge of the truth, there remaineth no more sacrifice for sins, but a certain fearful looking for of judgement and fiery indignation . . . ''

Lil knew where the fiery indignation was being felt, but while she groaned repeatedly, she refused to let further cries break from her throat.

The sound of the open-handed, stinging slaps overlaid the ribald voices that egged Creede on. Some called for a cane to be fetched. Some suggested, half-seriously, enactment of lurid fantasies in place of orthodox punishment.

Lil had lost count of the smacks long before he relented and let her up, to a smattering of hand-clapping and mocking cheers. She got quickly to her feet, letting her skirts fall to hide her warmed and smarting rear from the oglers. She was sure it must be a glowing red; tingling heat was spreading right through her lower body. Her untied drawers also fell — to her ankles — so she stepped out of them, knowing that to pull them up might allow more glimpses of leg, more carnal knowledge.

They were swooped up immediately, claimed by a drunk as a trophy and souvenir of the occasion. 'The jackpot's mine!'

'Give yuh five bucks for 'em, mister!' another merry-maker cried.

'Ten!' called a third.

A boozy auction got under way amid fresh mirth.

Creede pulled out his rum and swirled a measure around his mouth before swallowing.

Lil's thoroughly spanked bottom hurt sorely and she seethed at the mortifying exhibition the major had made of her.

'I'll get my own back, you see if I don't,' she told him, crimson-faced and watery-eyed but shedding no tears. 'You'll pay for this!'

'Well I never!' the Reverend Fisher said, blinking in the face of her fury.

Creede put away his flask, blew on his open right palm and laughed.

'I don't see how. While I cool my hand, you can study on how to cool your temper and tame your unruly tongue.'

'I'll see you in hell, bastard!'

8

Paid in Full

It seemed doubtful the ball at Fort Dennis could afford any excitement more irregular than the spanking of Lilian Goodnight, but alcohol continued to run freely and its consumption encouraged various semi-inebriated parties to retire from the main scene, as might be expected. Sometimes they went in twos, seeking privacy.

Not in their wildest imaginings did anyone suppose the biggest sensation was yet to come.

Jackson Farraday and Lil took the air in a quiet corner of the parade ground, shadowed by the stockade catwalk.

'A fat lot of use you were to a girl,' Lil said bluntly.

Jackson gave her the straight of it.

'No one with brains would've taken

115

cards in your silly game of ridiculing the general. I warned you against being headstrong. What could a man do? Start a fight with high-ranking men from Washington? It would've been better if you'd carried on acting like a young lady instead of just looking like one.'

'What he did to me was downright indecent!' she said.

'After you'd miscalculated the general would wear your sass.'

'Well, Major Creede had better watch out. I'm not gonna take it lying down — you can count on that.'

In truth, Jackson knew she was right to complain and that he must be sounding harsher than he felt. She'd been cruelly shamed, which was more than she'd been due. She'd have hurt feelings to nurse as well as the wear and tear on her hide. It was a wonder the shocking experience hadn't caused her to lose her self-possession completely. He figured she had to be more upset — no, because she was Misfit Lil, more enraged — than she wanted to let show.

'The women in town will all leer at me now,' Lil regretted after a short, reflective silence. 'They'll reckon they know things about me they didn't before. And the dirty-minded men will be bolder in their approaches than ever.'

'I can't argue with that. When the charms of a girl your age are made to look available, such is liable to happen.'

Jackson couldn't reassure her with denials. He'd seen the men's flushed faces. He'd heard unexpected words from the women of the company: in particular, from those who'd been drinking more freely than they were accustomed. Uncouth observations had issued from the mouths of respectable matrons who, on the morrow, on the town's main street, would probably meet him with demure looks and virtuous countenances and expect him to lift his hat politely.

With him, the whole incident would continue to rankle. How long would it take before the gossips and the sporting gentry of Silver Vein forgot to associate with his young friend the image of her pert rear patterned ingloriously with crimson hand-prints? How long to the day when gun-savvy Misfit Lil would claim retribution for the indignity she'd suffered?

'Maybe I should take you home to your pa's place,' he added, though he knew the Flying G was nowhere she'd want to crawl back, since she'd need at the least to apologize for past disgrace she'd brought upon the family name.

'Huh! Don't think I need any shoulder to cry on. Not even yours! I'd prefer to suffer my injuries alone.'

In a dark mood, Lil stormed off into the darkness and Jackson let her go.

That her spirit survived in belligerence brought a gathering of anxious creases to his forehead. Lil could be a sneaky young devil. She would get back at Creede somehow, maybe in a way no one could predict. And how would the next run-in end?

Jackson built a cigarette and drew on it, thinking long and hard. Bad times had come to Fort Dennis for a fact. Tonight's jollity and its meaner side brought the state of affairs home to him. The arrogant pair from Washington would ride rough-shod, not caring what or who was damaged in the process. He feared that giving offence to Colonel Lexborough's wife and effectively assaulting Misfit Lil were no more than trivial preliminaries in their agenda of self-aggrandisement.

Many long minutes dragged by and he lost track of the time. He didn't feel like socializing any more and kept his own company till the word was spread that supper was about to be served in the mess-hall ballroom. He crushed out his cigarette and joined a throng of folk returning to the organized festivities.

He wasn't the only one less than happy.

Fanny Kennedy had a reddened eye and what looked suspiciously like a bruise on her jaw; either she'd over-indulged on hard liquor and fallen or she'd been privately beaten by her husband, or both. Tom Kennedy wore a worried, guilty look.

Colonel Lexborough was stiff and unsmiling. His wife, Geraldine, was still the polite hostess but the front was clearly strained.

Lil Goodnight, uncommonly quiet, held well back from the centre of activity, pressed against the wall of plastered stone. Maybe its chill passed through her lovely ball gown and petticoat to ease a residual, throbbing heat in her smitten parts. She appeared tolerably more subdued since he'd last seen her, therefore unlikely to deliver more ill-considered outbursts against the 'distinguished' visitors.

General Morgan, looking like a strutting peacock with a fat behind, cast beady little eyes around the room. Jackson thought that, though powerful sure of his superiority to all the surveyed, he wasn't at ease.

'Where's my adjutant?' he demanded of the sycophantic group flanking him.

'Major Ezra Creede, sir?' a lieutenant said weakly, dismayed that he couldn't produce the answer.

'Who else, you damn fool!'

'He — er — said he was going to his quarters, sir.'

'What the hell for?'

The lieutenant trembled in his well-polished boots. 'I believe he mentioned having an assignation,' he said sheepishly.

Morgan was well into his cups. 'If you mean the major said he'd found a woman to poke, say so,' he said crudely. 'Go fetch him, man! I want him here when I give my speech.'

Jackson, intrigued, slipped out of the hall and followed along in the lieutenant's footsteps. So also, ahead of him, did Miss Wadsworth, the nosy president of the ladies' temperance society. Perhaps she hoped to learn the identity of the woman who'd granted Creede her favours.

The interest seemed kind of ghoulish — was that the right word? — to

Jackson. Who would want to accommodate such an obvious bully? The unfortunate woman, whoever she was, had to be drunk. For Miss Wadsworth to take advantage and spy was another of the night's unfairnesses.

The door to the room allocated to Major Creede in the officers' living quarters was ajar. Hearing no sounds within, and seeing a lamp burning, the lieutenant pushed it open and stepped through.

Then Purity Wadsworth let out a piercing scream. Whatever she saw over the lieutenant's shoulder, 'ghoulish' suddenly seemed to have become the appropriate word.

'Omigod!' she shrieked. 'He's dead!'

She turned and pushed past Jackson in an unseeing panic. Hitching her skirts clear of her slippered feet, she rushed back the way they'd come yelling, *'Murder! Murder!'*

The lieutenant backed out of the room.

'Better get a doc real fast . . . ' he

suggested, white at the gills.

'Hell, what's happened in there?' Jackson rapped.

He went in. The room was stuffy and smelled of lamp oil, sweat and spilled blood.

Ezra Creede was on the floor beside the iron-framed cot. He saw instantly why the sober Miss Wadsworth had gone to pieces and why the lieutenant hadn't the guts for it. A wound in battle was one thing: this was something else, altogether more shocking and macabre.

The major's pants and longjohns were in a heap alongside him. He was stretched out on his back in a dark pool of red, eyes open and staring, mouth twisted in a rictus of last agony. He still had one hand to the monstrosity at his hirsute groin; the other was a claw reaching for his chest where he'd been stabbed in the small vulnerable triangle just under the rib cage.

It hadn't been neat or efficient. He'd first been cut bloodily in the throat and the blade had been ripped downward cutting tunic and shirt. It had finally been driven deeply in, piercing his heart, completely burying the sharp, bright, slender shaft of steel.

But the golden hilt of the murder weapon stuck up and was clearly limned in the flickering lampglow. The feet of the proudly naked little goddess were planted in an ooze of blood; the red garnets at the points of her breasts twinkled like tiny fires, the only life atop a dead man.

It was the Medici dagger, beautiful but sinister, put with a deadly thrust to its originally intended use.

Fetch a doctor? Jackson didn't think so. Major Creede was a job for the undertaker. For all his crimes — of which Jackson didn't doubt there'd been many — he'd paid the price in full.

★   ★   ★

Horror and consternation erupted in the ballroom when the news brought by the hysterical temperance spinster was confirmed. Major Ezra Creede had been murdered! It spread through the room like wildfire.

'Well I never!' said the Reverend Titus Fisher. 'Well I never!' Mindful of the effect on his status of imbibing spiritous drink in public, he carried a cup in a saucer. It rattled nervously.

'More tea, vicar?' Lil asked meekly, fixing to sound like a lady from a long way east of the Mississippi River.

General Morgan, though shocked, was more affronted than upset by the death of his valuable underling.

'It's a calculated blow to undermine my authority!' he thundered at Colonel Lexborough. 'I demand an immediate call of the garrison to full alert! Guests are detained in the hall until further notice! Guard the doors!'

The general buttonholed Sheriff Hamish Howard as the representative of the civilian law. Jackson shook his head sadly at Lexborough.

'He's a mite pushy . . . high-handed.'

Lexborough was grave. 'Well, has anybody got a better notion? It's clear we have to start an investigation on the spot.'

Howard was nothing loath to give the general full co-operation. Obsequiously, he initiated searches and the questioning of all non-army men present. Colonel Lexborough was to supervise a similar interrogation of the soldiery. It fell to Mrs Lexborough to examine the women.

'What are we looking for?' Lieutenant Covington asked.

The colonel informed him that Creede had been stabbed with the Italian dagger presented to his wife, and its crimson velvet sheath had not been found at the murder scene.

'Gerry put the dagger in her reticule and she confesses she knew it had been purloined during the evening. She didn't want to make a fuss and spoil such an important occasion, so she said nothing. The general figures the murderer might still have the sheath on their person.'

'Damned stupid if they did,' Jackson

muttered under his breath.

To Jackson, Gerry admitted she'd thought the dagger, though unforgettably beautiful in its craftsmanship, a repulsive gift. When she'd handled it, a chill had fingered her spine.

'I would have been glad never to see it again!' she said, shivering anew. 'It was made for a Medici assassin.'

Howard's deputy, Sly Connor, pasty-faced and sweaty, was soon riled by the terse and bitter answers he got to his questions of the towners. Many were offended at the suggestion they could be suspects.

'*Me*, Deputy Connor?' the Reverend Fisher piped. 'Well I never!'

Connor was exasperated. 'What's the point of this tomfoolery, Sheriff? We all know who killed Creede. She told us her ownself she aimed to make him pay. Said she see him in hell! Most ever'body heard her say it.'

'Yuh're durn tootin' they did, Deputy!' Howard said, scowling. 'I know this is army property, but soon as Misfit Lil showed up here, I should've been asked to serve a Notice of Removal.'

Jackson said, 'What a stinking, pompous, good for-nothing jackass you are, Howard!'

The two peace officers ignored him.

'Waal, thing is. Sheriff,' Slv Connor said, 'has Mrs Lexborough searched the bitch yet?'

The exchange was conducted at a volume where it could be heard in many parts of the hall.

Lil continued to say nothing. Jackson considered it showed great restraint on her part. Maybe she'd taken to heart the advice he'd given her to behave like a well-mannered young lady.

'I have, Mr Connor,' Mrs Lexborough said calmly. 'Miss Goodnight has acquired no dagger sheath since we were all obliged to witness for ourselves — disgracefully, I might add — that she was hiding no weapon. She does, however, now have a belt and pistol under her skirts which clearly weren't there before.'

Connor said thinly, 'Heeled, huh?

That's suspicious.'

'But not the evidence you're looking for, Deputy,' Jackson spoke up again, electing to argue strenuously in Lil's defence. 'Might as well be self-protection for a girl whose underwear had been stolen.'

Howard stared in disbelief. 'Yuh're sayin' she's wearin' a gun cos she ain't wearin' drawers?'

But Jackson, though realizing how weak it sounded put so ludicrously, forged on.

'I don't believe Lil Goodnight would lure a man into some kind of rendezvous and stab him with a sneaky foreign dagger, if that's what you're charging. It isn't her way. Maybe someone's used her, framed her.'

The Reverend Fisher coughed. 'She was out of the hall a long spell.' He made it sound like he was uncovering a grave sin.

Lil broke her silence briefly but very coolly. 'So were lots of folks.'

'She was with me some of the time,' Jackson said.

Howard sneered. '*Some* of the time . . .'

The general said testily, 'Stop the palaver and get on with enquiries!'

With sullen grumblings, the Silver Vein lawmen reluctantly returned to what they reckoned was the farce of interrogation and search.

Jackson was accosted by Lieutenant Covington. He had the air of a man on a promising trail, inspired and eager.

'How did Miss Goodnight arrive here? She came by herself and met you here, didn't she?'

'Sure, she came on her grey and left it in the stables.'

'Then I'm going to check out that horse and its saddle gear right now,' Covington said. 'She had to get the gun rig from somewhere, which proves she was probably over to the stables sometime recent.'

He spun on his heels to go.

'You better look through the train of buggies and carriages everyone else has waiting out there, too!' Jackson flung after him.

When Covington returned, only

minutes later, breathless and triumphant, Jackson's heart sank to his boots.

'Misfit Lil's horse has been saddled up, ready to ride!' he accused loudly. 'And in a carpetbag tied on behind. I found this — tucked inside the roll of her buckskin clothes!'

With a proud flourish, he produced the distinctive red velvet sheath of the antique dagger.

'Well I never!' blurted Titus Fisher.

'Can't be no doubt about it now.' Howard declared, his evil mind working overtime. 'The vicious cat had her reckonin' with the major. Mebbe kidded him she'd gotten the hots from the wallopin' an' was point of fact invitin' him to have his way, then killed 'im fer what she was dealt fair an' square. She's guilty as hell!'

General Morgan roared, 'Arrest the whore! Makes no difference the culprit's a female. A murderess should dance on air at the end of rope!'

His face was empurpled with raw hatred.

9

A Clear Trail

Misfit Lil, meanwhile, had contrived to work herself toward the door. Only Deputy Sly Connor stood between her and the refuge of the dark night — and she had little fear of an oaf so slow and unimaginative. She was damn sure he was one of those strange men who were secretly scared of women and liked to pretend when they could that they didn't exist.

'It's all a set-up, you poor bone-heads!' she chided. 'No way would I've touched that filthy dagger. I wouldn't soil my hands on anything that'd belonged to George Hamilton Morgan — I've too much self-respect! It's a lousy business, but you'll have to learn the hard way, I guess: I'm innocent as a new-born babe.'

Howard snorted. 'Yuh sure didn't look like no new-born babe coupla hours age, an' yuh sure don't now!'

Connor let his hand drop for his gun. 'Raise your mitts, Lil Goodnight!'

But, lightning-fast, Lil dipped and raised her skirt with her left hand, revealing a split-second's flash of stockinged leg, fancy garters and womanhood. With her right, she hauled out the pistol from the belt over her naked hips.

The six-shooter was levelled and roaring before Connor, eyes bugging, had dragged his gun half out the holster.

Lil's shot ripped through the deputy's sleeve and fleshy upper arm, spinning him around clutching a blood-spurting wound. He crashed to the shiny waxed floorboards where he lay whimpering like a kicked cur-dog.

Lil swept the crowd with the gun firmly grasped in her hand. The smoke curled from its dark and menacing eye.

'*Freeze!* If anyone thinks they can

draw faster than I can crook my trigger finger, let 'em try!'

'Take her!' barked Howard, beside himself. 'Take her!'

But he didn't draw his own gun and no one else had the spunk or craziness so much as to think about it. Few Silver Veiners or Fort Dennis servicemen were not familiar with the reputation of the Princess of Pistoleers. She was hell on wheels with a six-gun. Moaning Sly Connor was merely a reminder.

'Listen, Sheriff *Coward* — and listen good!' Lil warned. 'I only winged Connor. Follow me through this door and you won't rig another election. You'll be electing to be a dead hero!'

Lil went out. She fired three shots into the lintel to deter anyone thinking of finding their courage. The bullets ricocheted with angry whines; stone splintered. Dust and gunsmoke swirled.

She ran to the stables and Rebel. She patted her faithful horse's head, tightened the cinch, and again hoisted the hem of the fancy ball gown's skirt to her waist. Long-legged and bare-thighed, she stepped into the saddle.

She put Rebel into a gallop for the open gates. The sergeant rushed from the guardhouse, waving her down with a sharp curse of annoyance.

'Whoa! What's the all-fired hurry? Where d'you think you're going?'

'General Morgan's had a heart attack!' she bluffed. 'Doc Craille says to ride lickety-spit to the druggist's store in town and fetch medicine!'

The sergeant hesitated. It was vaguely plausible. Lil and her horse were a combination to beat for speed.

'What was the shooting over to the mess hall?'

'It was just firecrackers!'

'Didn't sound to me like no — '

But Lil sent Rebel storming past him, forcing him to jump clear and enveloping him in a cloud of dust from the hard but worn path though the fort's entrance.

Within minutes, her guilt surely proven, she was riding away from the fort along the only trail that awaited her — the outlaw trail.

★   ★   ★

A council of war was under way in the mess hall, where the coloured streamers and bunting looked more incongruous than ever. Jackson Farraday found it hard to disagree with what was being said. Misfit Lil's flight made her situation look black, though he still didn't believe she could be a cold-blooded seductress and murderess.

'Hell of a note!' General Morgan complained sourly. 'My campaign not started and I'm upstaged by a murder! This has gotta be cleaned up fast before it becomes fodder for the more sensational Eastern papers.'

Jackson wondered if he really gave a damn about the grisly fate met by his aide.

Morgan swung on Sheriff Hamish Howard.

'This is a case for civil law enforcement.

136

I won't commit the army to hunting down a wretched female low-life. The troopers can't be spared. All Colonel Lexborough's establishment will be retraining to go up against Angry-fist's sub-tribe. Deputize, Sheriff! Raise a posse!'

'Why, sure, General, sure,' Howard said, falsely hearty but miserably aware he was being forced into doing some real lawdogging for once. 'We'll be on her trail at sunup. She can't get far.'

Jackson said. 'I don't know about that.'

But he didn't let the reproof sound as contemptuous as he felt. A few hours was maybe all Lil would need to show the clodhopping sheriff a clean pair of heels. And deep down he was still sure Lil was no tricky knife-killer.

'What do you mean?' Morgan said sharply, put out by the contradiction.

Colonel Lexborough tried to smooth matters. 'Miss Goodnight was born in this country. She's an expert rider and knows the terrain very well. She has the competence to go a long way in a few hours and to hide her tracks, too.'

'Goddamnit! She's only one *gal*, albeit full of sass and a dirty little killer.' Morgan blew down his nose in disgust. 'If the sheriff here don't do the job, I'll see she's captured myself when we go into the field to destroy Angry-fist.'

Tentatively, Jackson said, 'We still haven't any witnesses against Miss Goodnight, any real proof — '

Howard, determined to turn the fire on anyone but himself, got curt with him.

'The hell yuh say! It's plain as the nose on your face. The facts back it up. It was Misfit Lil who murdered Major Creede all right. We all saw the way of it: the filly got uppity; she got her needin's; she figured she had call to a stick a knife in the man who gave 'em her. 'Sides, she cut an' ran — don't that tell us she's guilty as sin? We don't need no more proof than that.'

'Like hell we do! No jury but a crooked one would convict a person on such flimsy evidence.' Jackson shook his head. 'Not in a million years.'

Howard's face was thunderous. 'It's enough for me!'

'It's enough to mean she's got questions to answer. I'll settle for that.'

Morgan had had enough of the argument. 'Blast it. Mr Farraday! Let Sheriff Howard moderate this and get it under control. He's the lawman here, man!'

Jackson knew Howard was useless at moderating or controlling anything — that was, short of the corruption in local politics and his own little, not-so-secret society of sycophants in Silver Vein. As Lil had once forthrightly put it, 'Howard don't amount to anything much and does damn little to earn his paydirt. County would be just as well off without him as with him.' But Jackson bit his tongue.

'All right, we wait till first light,' he said. 'Fact, I'll volunteer to go along myself and help the posse find the girl's trail.'

This way, Jackson thought, he might

still somehow be able to save rash Lil Goodnight from the consequences of her baffling actions.

Howard sneered. 'Suit yuhself. Don't reckon we'll need no tracker anyways. She ain't got much of a start.' To Morgan, he said, 'You can count on it, General. We got the felon good as nailed.'

Jackson took comfort in knowing this was a shaky claim. The trail-wise young woman could lose herself in the hills better than any man in the room.

Next morning, it seemed to his dismay that he'd read it wrong. Misfit Lil had left a trail that was plainly visible even to the fool tin-star and his posse of largely inexperienced volunteers. By dawn's light, they could see the tracks through the long and damp grasslands which Lil had, to Jackson's mind, carelessly traversed.

She went via the Flying G, her long-suffering father's ranch, where no one doubted she'd probably helped herself to provisions and water for a getaway.

'No nevermind,' Howard said. 'She can only carry so much an' the stuff'll run out.'

'I guess that's true,' Jackson agreed. 'But the posse will run out of the same essentials.'

Howard grunted. 'Mebbe yuh're right and mebbe not. We'll prob'ly catch her afore that. Lookit, she's left tracks as clean as they can ever get. She ain't so smart after all, that girly.'

It seemed undeniable, and the fact didn't please Jackson one bit. What was Lil thinking of? The whole thing got crazier by the moment. He knew the girl about delighted getting herself into scrapes, but this was serious trouble. She'd need all her skills to pull herself out of it — yet it looked like she was using nary a one.

As they rode into the hills, they passed many sections where the shrewd hunted rider could have sidetracked through timber and rock jumbles, hence slowing anybody following by obliging them to check closely for sign.

The total absence of caution on Lil's part worried Jackson. He understood, as well as he understood anything in the wide range of frontier lore, the thinking of men on the run. He'd followed heaps of malefactors and come to recognize their slyness and the tricks they used to out-fox pursuit.

Nine times out of ten, he'd found the most desperate men paused to hide their tracks. Or they tried to. It was a sound bet the time they lost rubbing out tracks and making false trails was paid back twice over in the minutes their hunters wasted in figuring out the real story told by deliberately broken undergrowth, scratched rocks and replanted horse droppings.

Lil knew this, too.

But Jackson could swear the obvious trail left by Lil Goodnight was genuine. She was aware of the calibre of her probable stalkers and it would have been no huge bother for her to have employed some of the elementary fugitive outlaw tricks.

Why the hell hadn't Lil tried to throw off her hunters by obscuring her trail, let alone not planting a false one?

Jackson shook his head in private wonder. It didn't make a lick of sense. But maybe good sense didn't come into it, being overruled by stronger emotions, like anger, hate.

Hate! That was the way to describe what Lil must have felt toward Major Creede, General Morgan and the sniggering folks of Silver Vein. Maybe even himself.

The last was the blackest of thoughts. Being the object of her hero-worship was wearing, but he realized in this moment that her friendship and respect were both things he couldn't stand to lose.

10

On the Dodge

Misfit Lil had lit out from Fort Dennis hell-for-leather with the wind biting her face. Her dark hair streamed loose behind her head and the skirt of the ball gown, much the worse for wear and with a rip or two appearing, whipped about Rebel's rump.

Lil figured she'd be better off all round in her trail rig. As the horse charged across the flats, mane flying and long stride eating up ground, she twisted in the saddle and unpicked the lashings that secured the carpetbag behind her. She thought, trust Mike Covington to have been the one to discover the Medici dagger's sheath!

She might have bet on it, knowing the tetchy, acrimonious nature of their relations and his determination to

144

curtail her aggravation. Her smile was wry.

She pulled up in the shadows of the first stand of timber she came to. There she removed the once-fine feminine dress with few regrets. She gathered its damaged and dirtied folds in her fists, raised them to her waist and took the garment off over her head with crossed arms, tugging to pull the tightfitting bodice over the firm rounds of her small breasts. The cool night air raised goosebumps on the firm and high flesh where it was exposed by the low neckline of her chemise and made stiffened tips thrust at the thin fabric. She donned fringed buckskin jacket and leather-reinforced levis, feeling relieved and as comfortable as a rigorously punished posterior would allow.

The night was dark and a thin overcast of cloud diffused the light of the brightest stars, but Lil's eyesight was keen and practised and she was no stranger to the never totally sleeping land and its critters. She made out the shapes of cautious, nocturnal wanderers. Wood rats and other small rodents scuttled through the undergrowth; overhead, bats and hunting owls flitted ghost-like. The greyness of the sky, though heavy, was enough to etch the bulk of trees and brush against the dimly lit rangeland and to outline the far horizons.

Lil was at ease with all this in a way she hadn't been in the fancied-up mess hall at the fort.

Quickly back in the saddle she sat loosely, moving instinctively to her mount's rhythm, letting the sure-footed horse choose its path through the gloom. She kept an anxious eye peeled for signs of pursuit.

'Goddamnit! Where are you?' she asked aloud. Knowing the personalities involved, especially that of Sheriff Howard, she hopefully deduced the chase might not be on in earnest till first light. But there had to be a hunt for her . . .

Maybe the breathing space was to the

good. She went to her father's familiar ranch headquarters at the Flying G, entering the place like a thief in the night.

Knowing the nature of every stiff latch, dry hinge and creaking board since the years of a boisterous childhood, it was no great difficulty for her to gather up all she thought she might need. She packed supplies including several canteens of water. She dared to cut and build some thick beef sandwiches.

Nobody disturbed the quiet preparations. She dropped nothing and didn't open a drawer or cupboard prone to squeak. But she worked fast, aware that even by starlight a posse could be expected to ride here and check out for her.

When she left, she took Rebel through thick, dew-wet graze, making no attempt to conceal her passage. Her intended destination was the rough country, away from the rangeland and beyond the hills. Here, she knew she could hide out in a hundred square miles of arid, worthless lands, criss-crossed by gorges and a maze of twisting canyons . . . a vast wilderness she sometimes reckoned she was better acquainted with than the pattern of lines on the palm of her hand.

As the sky became a lighter grey with the first, false dawn, it worried her a mite that Sheriff Howard, soldiers or other unfortunates called upon to help apprehend her had not yet shown. She hoped it merely meant they were confident she couldn't escape them.

Riding into foothills, she figured in the early morning it was time for her to make a stop. It would give Rebel a chance to rest up before the posse showed. Though at a steady lope, it had been a long, tiring journey full of uncertainty and the need for a constant watch for the route's pitfalls that darkness hid from the unwary.

She left Rebel on a grassy meadow from which she knew he wouldn't stray, but she didn't unsaddle and made camp close by, below an overhanging outcrop of rock where she built a small fire.

She discovered she was more tired than she'd supposed and fell unintentionally — riskily — into a doze.

Seemingly scant moments later, she jerked awake suddenly and completely — as was habitual for her — when an alarmed scrub-jay began a harsh scolding. The bird, though not much more than ten inches long, kicked up a hell of a racket. It flew over her head, its white-to-buff under-plumage streaked with blue.

To a person used to sleeping out, sounds came in two kinds. One was the good and safe; this was the other.

Lil's gaze swivelled to a distant, low clump of oak she'd passed when she'd ridden in to her campsite. There, under construction, she'd spotted a jays' sturdy nest of twigs, moss and dry grasses. It was a foot or so in diameter and ten feet above the ground. From observation, she knew the female of the species built the nest while the male supposedly guarded her efforts.

The scrub-jay that had flown over her head had plenty of reason for his annoyance.

A large body of riders was passing the oaks, making no effort to keep their disturbing approach quiet. The glare of the rising sun gave them long shadows but she could pick out the figures of Sheriff Hamish Howard and Jackson Farraday leading the noisy party. Tracking her, for a man of Jackson's ability, would have been a simple job indeed.

And they'd seen her horse! This was cutting it fine; maybe too fine.

Howard pointed excitedly and roared words that echoed off the rock behind her. They were indistinguishable but had clear, hostile meaning. Into the bargain, he had at his back a small army of like-minded idiots ready to take drastic action.

She had no doubt about what to do next.

Deeply thankful for the scrub-jay's wake-up call, and full of self-reproach she didn't have time to work through, Lil kicked out the remains of her fire and sprinted for Rebel.

The crack of a rifle added urgency to the need to exit a predicament an eventful evening and a night's sleeplessness had brought upon her. Fortunately, the eager rifleman was a poor shot. Moreover, he was on horseback and the range remained considerable.

'You'll have to do better than that.' Lil said to herself. But the attempt showed at least one man was convinced she was a mad-bitch killer, needing to be shot on sight. It established they believed she'd murdered Major Creede and were serious — these had to be the facts.

A second shot whipped past Lil's head with a buzzing sound as she soared into the saddle at the end of her run. She thought she heard Jackson remonstrating with the wild shooter. Then she was away and the chase was on at last in earnest.

Howard jammed his spurs into a tired horse's flanks cruelly, closing the gap. The ill-used beast whinnied in protest.

'Pull up, damn yuh, missy!' Howard thundered at Lil. 'Won't make no nevermind to me if we takes yuh back across your saddle 'stead of sittin' in it!'

Having the fresher and better mount, and possessing sharper horseback skills, Lil drew ahead again satisfied the bait was taken. Now she had to shake the posse before it could carry out Howard's threat.

Rebel was rested and fleet enough to stay a jump or two ahead of his pursuers. She touched heels to the game bronc and raced across an increasingly rugged and higher landscape, leading a strung-out cavalcade toward the canyonlands.

When she glanced back, she saw she was pulling away from the dust raised by the main mob of the posse. Only Jackson Farraday had knowledge of this country that might surpass her own. No one else — certainly not Sheriff Howard who was more at home in a padded office chair than a saddle — would be a serious rival to the experienced civilian scout and frontiersman. And though she didn't, couldn't know, she *had* to believe Jackson was still a friend, with enough trust in her innocence not to betray her when she made her final play to end the crazy chase. Otherwise she might as well give up now — and that was unthinkable.

Hunted and hunters stormed into a high, arid desert punctuated by weird formations: peaks, spires, pinnacles and arches framing patches of brilliant blue sky. The sandstone was mostly shades of red, though colourfully interspersed with cream and other pigments. Soon they were twisting and turning through a maze of ridges and narrow gullies where trapped heat made solid rock-faces shimmer.

If she could get through this section, Lil knew she could reach the place she wanted to go and effectively disappear. She could survive in the wilds for weeks — had done so happily in her chequered past many times.

Howard's posse would never get her. The canyons were a labyrinth of total confusion to all but the Indians and Jackson Farraday. Parched and hungry, the sheriff and his men would probably end up begging Jackson to lead them home!

But for now they were still powerful hot on her heels. She guessed that were it not for Jackson's restraining influence, the loco fools would already be cutting apparent corners, pushing their horses across the steep ridges instead of sticking to the winding trail ripping the hell out of the animals' stamina and leaving them with no reserves for the slightly better country ahead.

The trail took them several times close to the edges of dizzying drops into yet deeper canyons. Consequently, the pace of the chase had slowed somewhat before they reached a steep-sided basin of desert shrubland.

Again, she read omens in the activity of birdlife, but this time with quiet satisfaction and a proper measure of wilderness wisdom.

A hundred feet above, several birds circled in strongly undulating flight. They had wide wings and were roughly quail sized. Lil identified them as the burrowing owls she'd observed on previous visits to the basin. Unlike most other kinds of owl, these birds were busy day or night and in her mind she had them cast to play a part in a clever scheme to confound the ignorant posse.

The owls had a nesting site in a prairie-dog town abandoned by the stout, ground-squirrel rodents who'd first excavated its complex of tunnels. About a dozen pairs of owls returned here every March to repossess the burrows and set up a breeding colony.

Standing lookout on one long, sparsely feathered leg, a member of the group was perched on the mound of dry dung collected to mark its burrow's entrance, mask owl scent and provide additional protection from predators. The owl spied Lil's intrusion into its domain. It fluffed up its brown feathers to appear larger. It dropped and rotated its wings and began to bob up and down.

Lil made a detour that missed the nesting site and put her surefooted grey on a dead-end course for what appeared to be a sheer cliff face reaching up to the rim of the basin. Only one steep, precarious path ascended the face, and it was blocked where a tenacious greasewood plant had established itself on the flat, dry slope. The spiky, many branched shrub stood erect to some eight feet, its bright green leaves curtaining a single, narrow crevice.

The near-perpendicular rockface, though banded red and buff, looked as solid as the wall of some ancient European castle; the dark, narrow opening behind the greasewood like a window designed for the shooting of arrows.

'The dumb kid's ridden herself into a

trap!' Howard exulted.

Blind to all the warning signals, the sheriff and his followers recklessly headed straight for her, cutting directly across the basin and startling the lookout owl into flight.

As Rebel picked his way along the narrow track that angled up from the basin's bottom, Lil realized she'd lost much of her lead. The rattle of the posse's hoofs on the firm ground grew loud in her ears.

Fittingly, it was Howard's horse that was the first to make a false step into an owl's burrow. Its right foreleg sank into the hand-sized, funnel-shaped hole with catastrophic results.

The horse somersaulted, pitching, Howard from its back. He crashed heavily on a shoulder.

'Goddamn, I think I've bust my collarbone!'

But his howl of anger and pain was lost in the pitiful screams of the stricken, thrashing horse as it struggled futilely to get to its feet. Other possemen, swerving to avoid a pileup, collided or came to similar grief.

Lil tutted at their fool conduct.

Chaos reigned. The disturbed owls, male and female, added to the ruckus. Though no more than pigeon-sized, they had a two-foot wingspan, long, strong legs with talons, and curved, yellow beaks. In defence of their nests, some made sounds mimicking the rasp of rattlesnakes. A few boldly chased and struck at the spilled riders. It wasn't comical.

One cursing posseman broke through and urged his mount up the slope after Lil. He raised his gun and it bucked inexpertly in his fist. His aim was off but the bullet nonetheless skimmed Lil's right stirrup.

She turned in the saddle. That was too damn close!

'Stay put, Misfit Lil!' the dangerous shooter roared, drawing ever closer and pointing his smoking Colt threateningly. 'You ain't goin' no place!'

11

Disappearing Act

Lil held Rebel's reins high with her left hand and supported her six-gun over her stiffened forearm.

'So help me, mister — you've asked for it!'

She aimed at the bottom of her target, not the centre, knowing the muzzle would come up a little when the gun was fired. She squeezed the trigger, didn't jerk it.

The result confirmed her shooting superiority over the posseman who'd dared to fire at her. Not for nothing was she dubbed the Princess of Pistoleers.

Lil's slug hit the man in the thigh and caused his horse to rear as he was in the act of triggering a second loose shot. He was spilled out of the saddle with a startled cry, followed by a scream of terror. Both horse and rider went sliding and slithering on loose detritus down the steep, narrow slope. Dust swirled blindingly. The man had a foot caught up in a stirrup and an ankle probably broken as well as a bleeding thigh.

Meanwhile, Sheriff Howard was back on his feet and clutching his damaged shoulder.

'After the hellion, Farraday!' he ordered. 'She's unseated me an' shot another of my men!'

Lil thought his first accusation a stretch of the imagination — Howard had chosen to ride across the unsafe ground himself — and the wounded posseman had fired first.

It was music to her ears when Jackson said, 'Get her yourself, Howard! I'm about fed up to the teeth with these greenhorn plays.'

But all this Lil caught only in snatches. Reaching the tangle of the greasewood, she dismounted.

At close quarters, the crack in the

cliff the growth partly hid was shown to be wider than it had looked from the floor of the basin. The crevice must have been formed in a bygone time as a result of a unique combination of massive geological forces, probably including an underground shifting of strata and an above-ground erosion of a line of weakness.

While the men below struggled to sort themselves out, Lil smashed at the outer, spreading stems of the greasewood, breaking off green leaves and white and tan twigs, making it possible for her and her horse to proceed.

With coaxing words, she led Rebel between the greasewood and the rock: into the dark, tight passage of the fault . . .

★   ★   ★

Jackson Farraday put Howard's horse out of its misery with one well-placed, instantly fatal shot.

'That   was   kinda   rash,'   he   told

Howard, 'Your haste has lost us a good horse.'

The sheriff didn't deny his criticism.

'So what? We've cornered the murderin' wildcat, ain't we? She's gone inta that cave.'

Jackson opined, 'She might be in a good position up there.'

He took in the expanse of the basin with a flourish of a strong, tanned hand.

'This is open ground with scarcely a scattering of rocks big enough to give a jack-rabbit cover. Less'n we can squeeze into owls' burrows, she could cut us all down if she chose. She still has Dan Kennedy's rifle.

He paused to let Howard take the suggestion in; to imagine the lead whining and screaming about them.

A small, anxious-looking man from the disorganized party looked around at his sorry fellows, noting the number already injured.

He mumbled, 'We all know now for sure it was her killed Major Creede for punishin' her, Sheriff. She ain't apt to come quietly. I want no part of her.'

'Our friend here talks sense,' Jackson said.

But Howard scoffed. 'For God's sake, man, she can only have so many cartridges! I still say she's trapped herself.'

Jackson became evasive. 'I don't know. I ain't sure . . . '

The lawdog growled maliciously. 'She'll get thirsty an' hungry somethin' fierce sittin' in a dark an' hot cave with only a hoss fer comp'ny. Mebbe we jest gotta wait till she's outa water an' food.'

The posse was readier to side with him on that suggestion.

'Yeah, reckon we could an' should,' someone said.

Jackson knew differently, but he was the only one among the few present who were real, open-air men. He also knew the detail of the country. And he wasn't telling.

★　★　★

'I need a sawbones,' groaned the suffering posseman with the bullet-wounded thigh and broken ankle.

Apart from the complaints and the drone of a hot wind that swept into the basin from the canyons, nothing in two hours had relieved the monotonous silence of waiting for Misfit Lil to make her break from the crack in the rockface where she'd seemingly taken refuge.

Howard counselled, 'Let her get clear when she comes, so's she can't duck back inta cover when the gunfire starts.'

Jackson Farraday was appalled at his cold-bloodedness.

'I'd remind you she isn't proven guilty of any crime yet. She's just wanted for questioning.'

'I ain't never had no hots fer the bitch.' Howard lied jeeringly. 'I'd as soon cut her down as spit.'

Jackson Farraday gave him no further argument. content to wait as long as it took before the ornery sheriff realized Lil had outfoxed him. Then he aimed to play the innocent, feigning ignorance of her escape route.

It galled him, though, that his young friend hadn't somehow been able to alert him to what she was up to — whatever that was.

When Lilian Goodnight was in trouble, Jackson liked to think she knew she could confide in him and ask his advice. This time, accused of murder, she'd done nothing except behave in a way calculated to make everyone believe she was responsible for a crime of which he didn't think she was capable.

What was the truth about Major Creede? Did Lil know it? If so, why was she guarding against everyone else's knowing it? That everyone included himself rankled more than he wanted to admit.

Under the circumstances, it was difficult for him to speak up in her defence. She seemed to have done everything she could to cement the notion in the collective mind of the community that she was guilty.

To appoint himself her friend at the bar of public opinion would be a course full of fish-hooks. All sorts of accusations might be levelled. Her youth and beauty — the disparity in their ages — made it inappropriate for reasons that were personal, let alone out of consideration for the probity of his reputation.

The posse kept well back from the slope that led to the hole in the rock. Stares fixed on it. Faces were grim and uncertain. Respect for the quarry had deepened. Enthusiasm for the hunt had waned since Lil had tricked her followers into disarray and gone to ground in her high hideout. A few were tolerably unscathed, but the rest nursed cuts, bruises, swellings, abrasions and torn duds. The rashest, most battered had a bullet in his upper leg.

They were a doleful pack of *hombres*, Jackson thought.

The blast of the sun finally became unendurable and thin patience snapped.

'Aw, hell, we can't let the gal have us

treed!' Howard grated. 'What'll Gen'ral Morgan think of us? Them newspaper friends of his'll make us the laughin' stock of the nation when it gits out. Ain't like she's some noted curly wolf. Jest a dirty li'le whore an' man-killer!'

Jackson didn't rise to the irritating bait of the gratuitous insults. The only significant crime he recognized in Lilian Goodnight was awkward hero-worship of himself.

'You got something in mind?' he asked gently.

'Yeah! Fine lotta help you been, trailsman! Since yuh ain't got the nerve to do it. I'll have to go up thar an' root the bitch out my ownself.'

Jackson wondered why anyone should think apprehending a suspect was his duty. The scornful Sheriff Howard had odd notions of the tasks of his office, centring largely on taxes fees and fines — particularly the cut of them allowable for his personal remuneration.

Howard sighed heavily and turned. He took a deep breath between his thin

167

lips and his swelling chest strained at his leather vest with its glinting tin star. He raised his voice.

'You men be sure yuh gimme coverin' fire, but don't shoot me in the back accidental!'

Jackson reflected briefly that if he shot Howard in the back, it wouldn't be accidental but a giving-in to temptation.

A pistol drawn and cocked, his hand hovering over the butt of a second, Howard stomped across the basin.

Breath was held. But not a flicker of movement hinted of a young woman waiting to leap out from the darkness of a hole in the red rock to face him, gun to gun.

Howard was an habitual, do-nothing coward. Forced into action of a kind for which he had no stomach, his gun-arm was trembling as he began a stealthy climb of the narrow gradient where the way was ultimately blocked by the obscuring grease-wood.

Jackson took vengeful pleasure in

imagining the sweat that would be streaming down his jowly face and lardy body.

'I'm takin' yuh in, Lilian Goodnight!' Howard snarled. 'Throw out your guns or git your needin's!'

Silence. Even the persistent hot wind seemed to hit a lull.

What did he expect? That she'd jump into the light, hands up and saying, 'Here I am!'

When Howard was within ten feet of the mouth of Lil's hiding-place, he drew his second gun.

'This is your last warning! Come out, wherever yuh are! Else I'm fillin' your stinkin' den with lead!'

Increasingly nervous, Howard gave no time for any response to his final demand, but began to fire into the opening. He rapidly emptied the first gun.

Lead spanged and ricocheted off the rocks. The air was filled with whines and echoes, and swirling grey gun-smoke and red dust.

The gasping possemen watched on, ready to augment the cacophony the minute the murdering miscreant stumbled into view through the clouds, presumably with a gun of her own blazing at their 'brave' sheriff.

Nothing like it happened. Lil didn't appear and her surely terrified horse didn't start squealing.

Howard lost count of his shots and when his first gun clicked dully — metal on metal as he triggered, the chambers empty — he lifted the second and repeated the whole exercise.

Still Misfit Lil didn't stagger out.

As the reverberating clatter died, Jackson cleared his throat and called, 'Maybe she ain't there, Sheriff.'

'Whadyuh mean, ain't thar? She's prob'ly riddled . . . shot dead on' torn up to doll rags!'

'Better go on in and see.'

But Howard wasn't game till he was backed by several possemen armed with still-loaded guns. What they found when they stepped with trepidation through the crevice screened by the broken greasewood was the unexpected.

The assumption Misfit Lil had come to the end of her trail was wrong: they discovered what Jackson had known all along.

The dark, narrow cavity in the rock face through which she'd disappeared wasn't the entry to a shallow cave or cul-de-sac. It was the first turn of a passage that dog-legged deceptively through the twisted rock.

Howard was beside himself with fury. 'Goddamnit — empty! She must've gotten away while we were lyin' in wait out thar.'

'Likely she did,' Jackson said, nodding soberly, innocently. 'But who was to know?'

Nobody answered and though Howard's lips curled with the suspicion that Jackson himself might have known, he thought better than to make a case of it. He savvied the first result would be to underline his own ignorance, and it never served to expose inferiority in front of citizens and voters.

'C'mon, men! We gotta nail the bitch at all costs. She's hidin' out someplace through here. The gen'ral gave us the chore an' I ain't lettin' him down!'

* * *

When Misfit Lil had entered the passage leading her nervous range pony, she'd found it hot and stuffy with no light visible ahead beyond a faint glimmer that reflected off gloomy walls and outlined sharp corners. But a draught of warm air on her face told of an exit at the far end that she remembered from earlier exploration.

At its midpoint, the passage widened into a cavern. Here, a shaft through the high roof showed a small disc of the sky outside. A bat in a dark corner was woken by their arrival. It flapped past their heads on leathery wings and Rebel snorted disapproval.

The light from the natural chimney

illuminated a panel three times Lil's height and extending the length of the cavern. It was covered in drawings: humans, buffalo, deer, pronghorn antelope, bighorn sheep, shields, scorpions, dogs and a large beaked bird.

When she'd first seen it, Lil had been astounded by the wealth of the primitive art. It was before her pa had sent her to the academy in Boston, where she'd learned from a book in the library about the pictographs and petroglyphs of the Puebloan Indians. Petroglyphs were the graphics 'pecked' or abraded into the rock, probably by employing harder rocks as tools. Pictographs were the coloured representations painted on the rockface using plant dyes or mineral pigments.

From the pictures, it was plain the canyonlands had been a home to these ancient people and their culture; that they'd loved and respected the place and its wildlife just as she did. What had become of them? Where were they now?

The place was also unnerving, full of unseeable presence and a great and ominous sadness. But this visit, Lil had no time to breathe in what she thought of as the place's peculiar aroma of alien antiquity. She passed up the disturbingly heady experience and pressed on.

After more twisting and turning, girl and horse emerged from underground on to another canyon trail at the far end. The exit sat below a pinnacle of stratified red and white rock on top of which was balanced an enormous boulder, impressively precarious.

The canyon — it was barely more than a ravine — gave access to the far side of the mountain. Though it could be reached by other passes, it could be reached expeditiously no other way than that Lil had taken.

She now had a choice of routes. She chose one across hard, stony ground where at last she made every attempt to ensure she left no tracks.

12

Secret Valley

The gathering in the map room at Fort Dennis had all the happiness of a post-mortem, which is not much. Present were Jackson Farraday, Colonel Brook Lexborough, Lieutenant Michael Covington and Lieutenant-General George Hamilton Morgan.

The awareness of failure lay uncomfortably upon each with the exception of Jackson, whose sadness had other roots.

Morgan stood at the window that looked into the yard at the rear of the headquarters building where men were training horses in the sun. His hands were behind his back, and the fingers clenched and unclenched, a measure of his irritation.

'It rams home the folly of placing

trust in these hick-town peace officers,' he pontificated. He puffed up his chest which succeeded mainly in making his belly more prominent. 'A curse on no-good, bungling civilians!'

Jackson could have laughed at the inadequacy of the remark as applied to Sheriff Hamish Howard, but he didn't.

He said placatingly, 'The sheriff did empty two full pistols into what he thought was the suspect's hidey-hole, but she'd given us the slip and was already gone, leaving no tracks.'

The general's gash of a mouth twisted viciously.

'She should be back in Silver Vein . . . a corpse on display in a coffin outside the undertaker's.'

Colonel Lexborough, a man of restraint and wisdom, coughed and shook his grizzled head.

'Maybe it was as well Mr Howard's bullets were wasted. The shooting of a young woman out of hand would have had messy consequences.'

Morgan, after a second's glare,

misread the thrust of the observation.

'Of course! Good thinking, Colonel. Better to see the murdering trollop brought in alive and to book. She should be under lock and key, awaiting a show trial and hanging in public. Have to make it plain knifing high-ranking members of the military is not tolerated in a civilized nation!'

Lexborough refrained from pointing out that the sordid evidence likely to be produced at a trail would do little to enhance respect for the army.

The general mused a moment, relishing his imaginings, pig-like eyes narrowing.

'Never seen a woman hanged. Now that would be a memorable experience for the folks. Quite a revolting proce-dure. I believe.'

'But it isn't about to happen,' Jackson said.

Contempt was in his voice and his eyes were faraway, ice-blue and as cold as steel.

'Misfit Lil is a lost cause,' he went on.

'I don't reckon she stabbed Major Creede anyhow. I have to say, too, folks hereabouts know she speaks her mind. Being accustomed, they accept there's no sense in bothering about wounded pride. Frankly, Major Creede's public chastisement of Miss Goodnight invited retaliation, but it was no motive for murder. And we're not policemen. I thought we were here to plan the campaign against Angry-fist.'

Morgan's florid face drained of colour, then slowly began to redden again as the blood flowed back.

'Indeed, Mr Farraday,' Morgan huffed. 'But we shall accomplish both — the wiping-out of the renegade *and* the arrest of the murderer.'

Jackson was convinced of what he'd known before — the general was nothing if not muleheaded.

'Colonel!' Morgan barked, turning from the unsympathetic scout to the hapless fort commandant. 'I insist you spare a senior officer to be put in charge of finding the whore who killed

Major Creede. That she's still on the loose is a smear on my reputation.'

Colonel Lexborough, as always, had a full plate of problems without the over-arching, greater aggravation of General Morgan and his mission, doubly complicated by the violent death of his aide. Three soldiers playing cards in McHendry's saloon in Silver Vein had become involved in a drunken brawl and were presently incarcerated in the guardhouse; Corporal Kennedy was missing with his wife, Fanny, suspected of desertion after the disturbing death of his brother; an experienced sergeant — fit and healthy apart from stiffness from two old arrow wounds — had dropped dead that morning of an apparent heart attack suffered on the parade ground.

Moreover, Lexborough's beautiful, usually supportive wife Geraldine was upset by the passes Morgan persisted in making at every opportunity. The man was worse than a randy cow boy off a six-week cattle drive; he could scarcely keep his hands off her, it seemed.

In despair, but masking it as he had to, the colonel delegated the case of Misfit Lil to Lieutenant Covington.

All though the exchanges, Mike Covington had been standing by silently and dutifully, ramrod stiff and unflinching, the perfect picture of a West Point Academy graduate in clean and immaculate blue uniform.

'Mr Covington,' the colonel said, 'you're acquainted with the young lady in question. May I suggest it becomes your special brief to see that the matter is cleared up expeditiously and without undue disturbance to the army's normal, wider objectives?'

Though Lexborough broached it in a 'this is your mission should you care to accept' manner, it was obvious Covington had no choice.

'Yessir!' he clipped. He looked straight ahead and slightly up, avoiding meeting the glare of General Morgan or the persuasive gaze of the colonel.

Jackson felt for him. The lieutenant

had a mighty distaste for dealings with Lilian Goodnight, who delighted in embarrassing him. Jackson considered it regrettable on both their parts that they couldn't be more accepting of each other. With the right attitudes in place, they would make a handsome match. The child or children who inherited Mike Covington's pure, gentlemanly breeding and Lil's practical skills would go far and be an asset to any frontier community. But they remained blind to such qualities and possibilities, seeing only flaws in character and their petty disagreements. Lil had heaped scorn on Jackson's head whenever he'd ventured to act as peacemaker let alone matchmaker.

'Thank you, Mr Covington,' the colonel said with what sounded like relief.

'I'm obliged, Colonel, and will do my best to carry out my orders.'

Jackson had a new thought. Lexborough was sufficiently familiar with how it stood between Mike Covington and Lil Goodnight to know that his lieutenant, for one reason or another would be led a merry dance. Maybe the assignment would be enough to keep him safely out of range of whatever disasters General Morgan seemed so keen to precipitate. Maybe Lexborough actually had it in mind to do the eager young man a favour by effectively removing him from the mainstream of Morgan's dangerously faulty strategy. Jackson wasn't the only one who could see potential situations that might blight all their careers.

'Sir?' Covington continued questioningly.

'Yes, what is it?'

'An officer is only as good as the men he leads. I request a ten-man detail.'

Morgan looked like he might choke at the notion of a squad that size being diverted from the force that would be nominally be led by himself, but Lexborough forestalled objection with a swift, 'Very well.'

The flustered general, anticipating another wild-goose chase, could only add, 'Angry-fist and his band are the priority, of course. The uprising must be put down without further delay. If one bunch of savages gets away with it, whole tribes will walk off the reservations to go on the warpath.'

It sounded plausible, but to Jackson, who knew the red man, it was just so much drum-beating nonsense in the service of Morgan's ambitious interests.

Lexborough merely nodded and said flatly, 'You're dismissed, Lieutenant.'

Covington automatically saluted and took a regulation step back for the about-face to leave the presence of his superiors.

★   ★   ★

Misfit Lil had set up camp in what was virtually a secret valley. It was an oasis in the high desert of the canyonlands at an altitude of 5,000 feet. The valley was a natural amphitheatre with a deep, irregularly shaped pool of blue water — a small lake — occupying its lower parts.

The water was supplied by an

artesian spring rather than the run-off of rainfall that could be as little as ten inches a year. It sustained a variety of stands of timber, ranging from tangled willows and rustling aspens to grotesquely shaped ponderosas where the outer, bleaker ridges were exposed to cold winds that could drop night-time temperatures more than thirty degrees. Its best features, from Lil's viewpoint, were its inaccessibility and a lush green meadow of grass, cropped only by bighorn sheep.

She had shade, water, food and fuel for her horse and herself.

When darkness fell, the place sprang to life. Then, rats and most other small desert rodents, skunks, foxes, bobcats, mountain lions and owls paid their visits.

Lil hunted — a cautious, shadowy figure with Dan Kennedy's Winchester. On her second day in the valley, she stalked the wild sheep — a flock that included two thick-bodied rams with huge spiral horns, three ewes with a lamb each, and some yearlings.

Maybe the bighorns had never heard a rifle before. They scattered and fled, leaving one yearling the victim of the single, accurately placed shot.

The girl skinned and butchered her prize. Wanted parts of the prepared carcass, except for a cut from a leg, she preserved by lowering them deeply into a part of the lake that was shadowed. She buried the offal, collected cones and the branches of a deadfall, and built an oven of rocks over the pit of a cook-fire.

Later, once she'd eaten, she felt very comfortable about exile in the mountains. She could live here happily, counting off the days till she judged it was safe for her to return to the environs of Silver Vein and Fort Dennis.

But less than a week after her escape into the wilds, when she was exploring anew the barren canyons that surrounded her sanctuary, she received a shock.

From a rocky outcrop, she spotted

two figures wandering in a dazed, lost fashion through the sunbaked jumble below. They zig-zagged; they reeled. She wondered if they were fully conscious. She knew she was seeing the signs of a familiar disaster. Many a greenhorn venturer into these parts died of dehydration.

She also recognized the pair she was seeing with the ghastly sinking of spirits that makes a chilly void of the stomach when careful plans are ended at a fateful stroke.

The lost people were Corporal Thomas Kennedy and his wife, Fanny.

13

Prelude to Action

The column rode day and most of the night, plunging deeper into the canyonlands in search of war-painted savages at the order of General Morgan and under the reluctant guidance of Jackson Farraday. The timetable was gruelling, unnecessary and unlikely to yield results.

They would be prey to exposure, desert fever and, finally, buzzards in a nightmare landscape of nature's sculpting.

Both men and horses were sweat-soaked and weary.

A sergeant rode up from a position by the colours — a ludicrous trimming — and addressed the general.

'Sir! The men are mighty dry. Can we permit them to open canteens?'

Morgan grunted. 'If we must, but we'll never get to sight the hostiles unless we cover the ground. I want to see us getting into some action!'

Jackson didn't try to tell Morgan that swifter, shorter reconnoitring forays in smaller groups might be more effective than this spectacle of supposed armed might. This way, they weren't going to get within spitting distance of any Indians who didn't want them to.

Hell, Morgan wouldn't let anyone tell him much of anything. He possessed all the smugness of a man who'd ridden rough shod over too many better people in his career to grant any man present to be his superior. In this, his attitude was remarkably similar to that of Sheriff Howard, who was also a man of no talent but astonishing self-importance as he'd lately demonstrated.

And Jackson was sick of the Gatling gun and the problems it raised. Morgan insisted on detours when the going got rugged, so his precious piece of artillery didn't get jolted into misalignment, its carriage buckled or the wheels broken.

'It's more trouble than it'll be worth,' Jackson had promised.

'Stick to your job, Mr Farraday,' the general had said curtly. 'Specialists view the Gatling as the instrument whereby we'll most efficiently achieve the major slaughter I envision. You shall see. It'll spell a major victory. My name will be emblazoned on the front page of every Eastern newspaper, mark my words.'

Jackson still seethed inside over the put-down. He'd prefer to see the whole, rattling kit-and-caboodle of Morgan's Gatling shaken to bits before they ran into Angry-fist. Why, they'd probably be sitting targets for attack while the devilish machine was being set up. Jackson would prefer to ride alone — answer to no man — than to be tied to General George Hamilton Morgan and his half-baked notions and theories. He had to work hard at not letting his distaste for the man develop into unmanageable hatred.

He schooled himself to think of other

people and wondered how Lieutenant Michael Covington was making out. His career was probably safe from the consequences of failing to please General Morgan, but he figured Misfit Lil would be playing the young officer for a sucker someplace, if he'd found hide or hair of her.

The girl was at home in the wilderness. He savvied she adored the grass-grown range, timberclad hills, the forbidding magnificence of the canyons and the quiet solitude of nature. She was never happier than when hunting, roaming around. Or working with horses and cattle, sipping fine whiskey . . .

He'd recently told her if she carried on living like a man much longer, she'd surely start growing whiskers. She'd told him he was starting to sound like her pa or Mike Covington and to shut up.

Where was she now?

★ ★ ★

Misfit Lil was badly shaken by the discovery of the Kennedys in this inhospitable country where she'd least expected them. They were in a state nigh on delirium and she couldn't get any sense out of them at first.

They were conscious enough of Lil to let her lead them into her valley hideout. She suspected, however, that they thought they were only dreaming she'd found them.

'I'm real,' she reassured them, fearing they'd dismiss her as an hallucination and give up their slipping grip on life. A few more hours and they would have been dead of sunstroke.

She bathed their sun-blistered faces and lips that were bloodily cracked. With the cloth, she squeezed water on to their swollen tongues, just a dribble at first, but more as their minutes in the shade passed.

'You mustn't drink too much right now,' she warned.

Lil's sick dread that they would die slowly abated, but not her concern at their presence. Nonetheless, it was a full hour before they could drink sparingly from a canteen. And talk coherently.

'You were meant to have deserted from Fort Dennis days back and to be halfway to San Francisco,' Lil reminded the couple. 'That was the plan, remember? More precisely, you were to meet up with a sea-captain friend whose windjammer plies the trade route across the Pacific to New Zealand.'

Tom Kennedy was a junior version of his slaughtered brother. Dan — thick-set, bullish.

'We ain't here deliberate, Lil. You dunno how hard it was. Colonel Lexborough had patrols out every-where.'

'S-sorry, Lil,' Fanny said in a small voice, brushing the thin strands of reddish hair off her face. 'We fouled up.'

'Naw, we didn't!' Kennedy said stoutly. 'We din' get a lotta choice, see? Howard's posse was prowlin' 'bout likewise — still hopin' you'd show, I guess. There was Indians lurkin', too. We had to give everyone the slip.'

'So you headed the wrong way completely,' Lil said, staring levelly at him. She didn't disguise she was dubious of the explanation.

'We kept gettin' *pushed* south, to dodge 'em. We couldn't risk swingin' back west.'

Lil thought for a minute, accepting the difficulty they must have faced, though she felt Tom Kennedy's pride left him incapable of telling all. Plainly, he'd become totally disorientated.

'But what happened to your horses?' she asked.

Fanny put on a shamefaced grimace. 'That was my fault. They got spooked in a freak lightning storm. I hadn't hobbled them properly and we lost them. I expect they galloped back to the fort.'

Lil shook her head slowly. 'Time's a-wasting. This is scarcely the place to be. I've seen Angry-fist's scouts moving in. They've gotten wind a big force of white soldiers is out looking for their blood. It's probably too late to put the original plan to save you back on track. Now I'll have to keep both myself and you hidden. That'll be a tough call.'

She knew she'd never get them back on the trail they were supposed to be travelling unless she guided them herself. Only she or someone like Jackson Farraday knew the endless canyon mazes thoroughly enough. Moreover, under present conditions, they were hardly likely to be left in peace to make the journey.

Kennedy shrugged and said stubbornly, 'You mind what I say, Lilian Goodnight. We're grateful to you more'n ever, but we didn't botch nothing. It was purely hard luck and we got plumb tuckered out, is all.'

For once, Lil didn't have the spirit to argue. In getting lost, the Kennedys had thrown away the best chance she'd been able to give them.

Lil was also no longer confident that she'd have the chance to save her own neck. What she had to do in the coming days would be very, very risky.

★ ★ ★

Michael Covington was puzzled by the tracks he was following. Tracking was not his speciality. He more usually left chores of its ilk to civilians paid to assist him. Men like Jackson Farraday. But Farraday's services had been appropriated this time round by General Morgan for his grand, headline-making mission to destroy the menace of Angry-fist once and for all.

Falling back on his own limited abilities Covington was aware he was following the tracks of a white woman accompanied by a white man. The tracks were too clumsily made for the woman in question to be his quarry — the pesky nuisance turned murderer, Misfit Lil.

He had wondered almost immediately whether they might have been left by the recent deserter. burly Corporal

Tom Kennedy, and his rather pathetic wife, Fanny. It was not in his specific brief to locate the Kennedys, and Covington was ever one for following orders to the letter, but he thought he had best try.

This was why he was high on a ridge, a vantage point that gave him a view of an unexpected, green valley toward which the tracks were trending. It was searingly hot in the noon sun. A shelving outcrop overhanging what passed for a trail offered a modicum of irregular shade near the top of the ascent.

Rising in his saddle, Covington turned on his small party and said, 'We'll rest up a spell, men. Let the horses blow. Circle and dismount!'

The troopers slipped gratefully from their saddles, loosened cinches that had been tightened for the long climb, and sought the relief of the shadows.

It was only when he'd dismounted and loosened the cinch himself that he noted the activity way below and in the shimmering distance. He reached for field glasses to check on the black specks creeping, insect-like, away from the valley to which he supposed the pair they'd been following were headed.

The specks and the trail they traversed were a thousand or more feet below, maybe two miles away.

As was so easily done when training glasses on small, distant objects, Covington missed his target first-off. He found his magnified gaze focused on bare rock. Sweeping across the rugged land to find what he wanted to study, he accidentally found other figures — intent, motionless and cunningly concealed among the boulders.

Indians!

'Damnit!' he exclaimed. 'There's a bunch of hostiles down there.' And then, as he anxiously swung the glasses to find the specks that had first caught his attention: 'Ye Gods! Corporal and Mrs Kennedy — and our fugitive, Lilian Goodnight. The three of them walking right into an ambush!'

The wily Indians had taken positions above the rough trail and had the drop on the trio. It looked like they were just waiting for the right moment to jump them. A scene of red, bloody slaughter leaped into his mind's eye.

He wheeled on his troop. 'Mount up! Prepare to move out!'

To a man, the weary horse soldiers were suddenly galvanized into life. They leaped for sweat-damp, uncooled saddles.

Astride his prancing horse, Covington drew his sabre.

'Forward at the gallop!' he yelled. 'Charge!'

The cavalry detail plunged pell-mell down the dangerous incline.

14

Thunder in the Canyons

It was not a position Misfit Lil would normally have gotten into. For several days, she'd seen evidence that Angry-fist's rebels were coming deeper into the canyonlands, ever closer to her hideaway, pushed thataway by the widening sweeps of the military. A showdown clash seemed inevitable.

By herself, with Rebel, she would have been ready to ride it out — or ride out. With the Kennedys' arrival, she was put between a rock and hard place.

The best move she could think of was to lead them out, find them transport and set them back on their way west, before consequences from the impending clash between the army and the renegade Apaches flushed them out and all was lost.

She'd no illusions it would be anything but a slow and dangerous trip, but she couched it in optimistic terms.

'I've heard of emigrants passing through headed for California. The regular trail is north, near the Salt Lake. A party might let you join them,' she told her unwelcome guests hopefully.

But she didn't think the breakout from the backend of nowhere was such a good idea after all when she sensed, in the uncanny way that seemed born and bred into her, the presence of Indians stalking the rocky slopes bounding their trail.

'Their eyes are on us — I can *feel* 'em,' she hissed to Kennedy and Fanny.

'Maybe this is a fool notion, Lil,' Fanny quavered. 'Maybe we should have stayed put.'

'And let the army stumble across us?' Lil said, scorning the suggestion. 'I don't fancy a hangrope around my neck! Anyhow, Angry-fist will see you aren't pony soldiers, and you're toting no tempting booty.'

Fanny wasn't reassured. 'They could be after taking our scalps, like they did Dan and Edith's. If they recognize you, Lil, they'll be sure to attack.'

Kennedy said, 'Could be wise to go back, make a defensive stand.'

Lil firmly disagreed. 'Well, I'm the leader and I say we're in no position. We'll carry on . . . leastways, as long as they'll let us.'

It was nothing Lil or the Kennedys did that precipitated the violence. The troop of cavalry came storming down the slope like the proverbial bats out of hell. Lil's surprise was spiced with anger as the faint possibility of continuing on their way unmolested evaporated.

Fanny's mouth fell open at the sight of the blue uniforms, led by the dashing Lieutenant Covington, who was the pivot of much fantasizing even among the young and not-so-young married women of Fort Dennis.

'We're saved!' she cried, forgetting these men wanted her guide for murder and her husband for desertion.

'No, we're not!' Lil rapped, disabusing her. 'Hunt cover, the pair of you! And fast!'

The soldiers cut loose with a ragged volley of gunfire. Bullets ricocheted from rocks in all directions. Through the rising puffs of dust, Lil saw at least three Apaches die as Covington's detail made its first run, aided by the element of surprise.

But it was not to be a one-sided battle. As the riders surged through the hostiles' positions, one Apache, sheltered in a nest of boulders, let fly with an arrow that hit a passing soldier square and forcefully in the back, knocking him out of the saddle. The cavalry horse carried on, dragging his body.

And the Indians were themselves masters of hit-and-run, perfected in numerous raiding sorties. They made swift use of the vital seconds they knew it would take Covington's men to turn their mounts for a second charge. The better positioned dived for cover among the less accessible rocks, where many had rested rifles. Others ran to where they'd left their mustangs and mounted up for a counter-attack.

'Confound you, Mike Covington!' Lil cursed. 'This serves no end at all!'

Covington's troopers circled round and made to repeat their pass through the redmen's lines.

'Send the lot of 'em to the happy hunting grounds!' someone cried, his bloodlust up.

But the tables were about to be turned in earnest. The shooting had been heard by a larger band of Angry-fist's followers. They dashed in on wiry ponies to join the fray now embroiling the potential ambushers of two white women with one white man.

Carbines spat fire in the brightness of the afternoon. The enthusiastic Covington and his men were caught between two forces of Apaches in a pincer movement.

Clinging to Rebel behind the largest

trailside boulder she could find, Lil was horrified.

'Crazy galoot! He's really put the fat in the fire!'

For the white men, nothing was feasible but to quit or die.

'Disengage!' Covington yelled abruptly. 'Snap to it — we're outnumbered!'

The soldiers wheeled their horses and put them into a run for their lives. One man's horse stumbled and fell, unseating him. He started running on foot, hatless, face white with fear as bullets peppered the dust at his heels.

But his Apache pursuers quickly outstripped him. Jeering and whooping they placed bullet after bullet around and in him, playing with his life. He yelped. In terror, he lurched first one way, then another. Lead kicked up dust all around his feet. He slipped down-slope, started to get up but stumbled into a complete somersault before he staggered upright to regain unsteady footing. Then a bullet hit him in the back of the head, doing horrific damage to his face. He was pitched on to it and lay still in a quickly forming pool of blood.

The gruesome fun and games gave Lil and her friends a slim chance before the Apaches remembered them.

Lil saw at least two army horses, saddles empty, unsure whether to stand on dropped reins or gallop after their retreating stablemates.

'Hold Rebel,' she told the Kennedys. 'I'm going to fetch those broncs — you need them!'

Tom Kennedy saw it as his place to give Lil a hand. Disregarding her instructions, he rushed out after her in time to cop a shower of stone fragments.

One Apache not involved in tormenting the trooper left behind had spotted Lil's movement and he fired quickly, missing but hitting the boulder behind. The bullet skimmed and shattered the hard surface, whining on in another direction.

Sharp splinters of rock tore into Kennedy's eyes.

He clawed at his face. 'I'm blind! I'm blind!' he screamed.

Fanny grabbed him and dragged him back into cover.

Lil managed to catch one army horse quick-smart and pulled it back to join them.

Fanny wailed in distress and panic. 'Oh, my God! Tom's hit! He can't see! What shall we do?'

'Get on the horse!' Lil ordered. 'I'll help him up behind you. You'll have to ride double.'

Risking their already imperilled lives, they took off hell-for-leather after Covington and his surviving troopers. Kennedy was close to passing out but somehow clung on to his sobbing wife.

Covington had drawn rein to regroup his depleted force and they caught up faster than Lil had hoped. His men were white-faced and shaking. Some were injured and doing their best to staunch bleeding wounds.

She rode up directly to the lieutenant, standing no on ceremony and butting into his orders to his men.

'Fat lot of good you did, Mike Covington!'

The men's eyes widened as though she'd just stepped from another world. Bold as brass, the murderess was not only without remorse but dressing-down their senior officer.

Covington was nothing if not stead-fast to his aims. Pulling his horse alongside, he leaned toward Lil to take her arm.

'Miss Lilian Goodnight, you're under —'

'Forget it, mister!' Lil blazed, shrug-ging free. 'We'll sort that bullcrap later. You let the Apaches catch you here and there'll be no arresting done — and no starch left to knock outa you!'

'Looks to me it's lucky for you we showed when we did!' Covington retaliated. 'You were in real trouble.'

'Which you didn't much help.'

'You're still alive, aren't you?'

A trooper put in morosely, 'For now. The red bastards are gonna git us all anyways!'

'They ain't!' Lil declared vehemently.

'I'd admire for you to tell us why they ain't, missy.'

'They got us outnumbered here, but I know a way through to the far side of the mountain the Indians don't or won't use.'

'I heard,' Covington said drily. 'Sheriff Howard has yet to live it down.'

'Well, what are we waiting for?' Lil said. 'Let's ride!'

★　★　★

Jackson Farraday heard the distinctive crackle of shooting echoing through the twisted labyrinth of the canyons. He was leading General Morgan's force on the trail of a large party of Indians. He immediately deduced that the Indians must have met up and clashed with the small detachment led by Lieutenant Michael Covington in search of the disgraced Misfit Lil in the same country.

'Time to proceed at the double,

General!' Jackson said. Turning in the saddle to the other officers, he said, 'Pass the order for everyone to hurry up!'

Morgan was not a natural horseman and was finding the going difficult enough.

'You over-reach yourself, sir!' he protested. 'I'll make the decisions here. If we go any faster, the Gatling gun could suffer damage.'

'Then the contraption has no place being here . . . God damn it to hell! We're a cavalry column, not the artillery.'

Morgan's face darkened. 'I've tried hard to like you, Mr Farraday, but God help you when we get back to Fort Dennis! You'll be through with the United States Army, I swear!'

As they slowed to argue, the experienced soldiers behind them, who had also savvied the increased urgency of their mission, swerved around them and went into a charge. Bugles blasted.

Apoplectic with anger, Morgan found

himself swept along regardless, striving to maintain a position in the van.

Jackson feared the general's prized Gatling gun was taking a severe pounding as it danced and hopped along behind, bouncing from rock to rock on its rigid carriage, rattling alarmingly.

He didn't care.

★ ★ ★

Misfit Lil led Lieutenant Covington's remnant search party into what appeared to be a box canyon.

'This is suicide, Miss Goodnight,' Covington objected. 'Do you want the rest of the troop wiped out — yourself and the Kennedys included? To die turning tail is a disgrace!'

Lil bit her tongue. She refrained from pointing out that her idea of a cavalry troop — especially one sent into country inhabited by hostile guerrilla fighters — was maybe sixty horsemen with two lieutenants and a captain, and that the odds had always been impossible. Retreat was Mike Covington's only option and no disgrace.

Keeping strictly to what had to be done, she pointed to the opening in the cliff face overshadowed by a spectacularly balanced boulder perched on a tall column of rock that looked like a manmade pillar but was the work of erosion on softer, surrounding material.

'You can escape through there, single file, leading your horses. It'll bring you out in a basin on the far side of the mountain.'

Covington frowned. 'I'm not happy this is as easy as you make it sound, but you've left us no other choice now. Angry-fist's warriors will be snapping at our rears any moment.'

'Get going!' Lil urged. 'You'll be safely through in five minutes.' With a bid to lighten the doom-laden atmosphere, she added flippantly, 'Just watch out then for the burrowing owls' nesting ground.'

Reluctantly, Covington ordered his

men to dismount and enter what looked like the very bowels of the earth.

The next hitch was when Fanny Kennedy dithered.

'I get claustrophobia in underground places. I can't go on! And Tom's hurt . . . '

Kennedy clutched hands to his bloody face and moaned. 'Can't see . . . can't do it!'

Covington snapped, 'Proceed, Corporal Kennedy! You're a prisoner already for desertion; disobedience of an order won't go well for you.'

Misfit Lil intervened, 'You go on, Mike. They're not going to co-operate with you and there's no time for bullying. Your men need you. Join them and I'll bring the Kennedys through myself. I give you my word.'

Covington's cards were all played. At a loss to know what else he could do, he complied with her suggestion.

Fanny looked round desperately for some other, non-existent escape route. She darted this way and that with whimpers of distress like a terrified ground squirrel. She looked up at the high, precariously balanced mass of the boulder, though she must have known no one could climb to its perch, least of all a blind man and two girls. Nor did it offer security — just a trap.

Then the Indians came into the canyon, firing carbines.

Lil seized Dan Kennedy's Winchester, which she'd been carrying in a leather loop attached to her saddlehorn. She levered in a round, twisted to face the oncoming riders, took careful aim and fired. An Apache instantly tumbled to the ground.

Lil worked the lever, firing as fast as she could with accuracy, but it didn't look like being enough to turn the wild bunch . . .

* * *

Jackson Farraday and the main body of General Morgan's party reached the rim of the box canyon containing

213

the opening to the tunnel through the mountain. As they did so, a new flurry of gunfire broke out, accompanied by the triumphant yells of confidently attacking Apaches.

'They're firing on Covington's detail again,' Jackson said. 'We're just too late.'

But he was about to witness a daring, seemingly suicidal act. He saw Misfit Lil throw down Dan Kennedy's empty rifle and jump astride her horse. She whipped out her six-guns, wheeled the grey around, and charged right into the ranks of the approaching Apaches.

Letting out several blood-chilling screams laced with profanities, she poured a stream of lead into the bronzed bodies, before slipping down over the side of Rebel, Indian fashion, and riding straight through the broken ranks. She reached safety beyond while the Apaches were still struggling to control and turn their squealing, half-wild mustangs.

Jackson jerked into action.

'She's won a chance. We'll ride down

and try to even the odds.'

'No, we won't!' General Morgan roared. He'd noted the other white woman tending an injured corporal by a hole in the rock. 'I do believe the rash sharpshooter is the whore who murdered Major Creede. We'll save the others. We'll get the Gatling down by the hole in the rock and mow down the hostiles when they regroup for a fresh attack.'

Jackson demurred. 'We'd do better to assist a tactical withdrawal. It's time for smart thinking.'

'We're not pulling out till the job's done!'

'Your way will cost many more lives on both sides.'

'We're not quitting! My way is the *American* way!'

Under Morgan's instructions, and not without difficulty and cussing, the Gatling was hauled and lowered down the steep slope to a position close by the bizarrely balanced boulder and its tall pedestal.

Jackson saw from the dull anger burning on most faces that the men were bitter as the company held off the Apaches to allow the job to be completed. Morgan's strategy was folly fatal to many of their number and it was of little consolation to know the Apaches were being set up for red, bloody massacre.

Finally, when the gun was in place, supposedly in defence of the cowering white couple, it jammed as the first wave of attack was allowed within its range.

The Gatling operator slumped back dead — an arrow in his chest.

Morgan uttered a sound which was halfway between a gasp and a strangled sob. He dropped down from his horse and began running toward his precious machine.

'Fools! Dumb heads!' he bellowed.

An Apache bullet tore through the side of his tunic without seeming to touch flesh beneath. He faltered — but only momentarily — then went on.

'Stop, you crazy galoot!' Jackson yelled. 'Get back!'

But Morgan ignored the call.

Frenzied, he leaped on to the Gatling's platform, gripped the trigger handle with his left hand, and began turning the crank with his right.

Somehow, the works unstuck. The Gatling's cluster of ten barrels churned round the central axis, spewing flame, smoke and lead in a deafening, continuous thunder.

The Apaches were ripped apart by the Gatling's deadly swathe. Men and horses fell, torn and bloodied. Jackson felt bile rise to his throat; he was unable to do a blessed thing to halt the slaughter.

But Morgan's luck deserted him. He was hit in the throat by a bullet. With a choking gurgle, he fell backwards and sideways, the wound spurting blood, his eyes glazing. Yet still his hands clung to the Gatling, working by reflex.

His life's miserable work wasn't quite finished.

The hail of undirected lead shot upwards and swung in an arc till it struck the highest part of the column of rock supporting the balanced boulder. There it fixed, hammering fist-sized chunks out of the weathered sandstone as the chattering gun kept rotating.

For a breathtaking moment, the monstrous boulder rocked and quivered like a live thing. A million years ago, glacial ice had deposited it on its perch, a megalith in defiance of gravity, a natural wonder attributed by the superstitious to gods, devils, giants, demons or fairies. Now the day had come for it to continue its journey.

The sandstone beneath the boulder cracked and crumbled. The boulder teetered. It *fell*.

It slammed into the steep slope above the entrance to the tunnel, smashing more brittle rock into pieces like eggshell. Other boulders, the debris of earlier slips, dotted the area. The mighty impact set them in motion with a rumble like an earthquake.

In panic, bluecoats and redskins fought their mounts to get out of the way of the apocalyptic phenomenon. The very land under them seemed to be sliding. The boulders bounced, crashed and crunched their way through the place where Morgan and the Kennedys were, burying both the dead and the living. They spilled across the canyon bottom, shattering other rocks already there, raising blinding clouds of dust so thick they filled the whole canyon and darkened the sky above for minutes.

At last, a breath of wind wafted the dust away. A grim, near silence descended and the sky turned blue once more.

Jackson drew a shuddering breath of the clearing air into his lungs. His senses reeled when he saw the carnage. He swore mightily and long, the grit grinding between his teeth.

15

What Really Happened

The surviving Apaches fled the scene in wild-eyed terror. The Gatling and the disaster it had sparked were merciless and effective in the rout of Angryfist's reservation defectors.

But the slip also blocked the tunnel entrance.

General Morgan's battered company began the trek back to Fort Dennis the long way — the only way — round the mountain, through thirtysome square miles of canyons.

'Keep your eyes skinned for Misfit Lil,' Jackson said.

They found Lil with her back against a stunted tree, binding up her forearm with a red bandanna.

'Hit?' Jackson asked.

'Nothing to speak of. Close though.

A bullet grazed my arm.'

She took in the troopers riding double; the slings and bandages in abundant evidence. Many faces were grey and drawn with pain.

'You all right?'

'I'm one of the few without a scratch.'

'What happened to Fanny and Tom Kennedy?'

'Dead, I'm sorry to say. When the balanced boulder fell, the ground slid from under them and they got buried by the tumbling rocks.'

'God, that's terrible.'

Lil was silent for a long moment, very thoughtful.

'Maybe it's for the best,' she said at last. 'Since they didn't get away, I don't know how it would have worked out.'

'Sure,' Jackson agreed. 'I've figured some things.'

'Mike Covington hasn't. He was still wanting to arrest me for Creede's murder when he took his men through the tunnel.'

Jackson nodded. 'His ordered mind

doesn't easily make the kind of jump that would have told him Misfit Lil was framed by Misfit Lil,' he said wryly. 'You put the sheath of the Medici dagger in your carpetbag yourself, didn't you?'

Lil, completing her first-aid, rewarded his guesswork with a rueful half-smile.

'Uh-huh. It seemed the only way to save Fanny after she'd killed the major. He'd deserved to die: she didn't.'

'But I still don't know what the killing was about, Lil. And Mrs Kennedy was such a timid and nervy young woman . . . I guess you have the whole story.'

Lil said she did, and that it was a long one.

'Give it me anyways — all! You know I don't like shilly-shally.'

Lil fixed her eyes on a distance that wavered in the heat-haze, took a deep breath and began.

★　★　★

'You have to go back to when Fanny was a button in Colorado. It was there that all other members of her family were massacred by the Cheyenne.

'The Indians hit 'em not because the family had done anything bad, but in swift retaliation for the slaughter by treacherous military of sleeping members of their tribe — mostly old men, women and children — who'd supposed themselves in safe custody, under the army's protection, on a reservation.'

Grim-faced now, Lil went on, 'The soldiers' attack, fifteen years ago, was covered up. It made no difference that they'd raped the women and girls, taken scalps and severed genitals. The crime was dismissed by men in high places who ought to have known better. Maybe they reckoned it was fitting treatment of lousy Indians.'

Jackson was tolerably shocked. 'A nasty business, but such atrocities are on record. History will judge the perpetrators.'

'With her parents and siblings all

dead, Fanny was brung up, fondly and lovingly, by her old mammy who hoped she'd forget the horror of the Indian attack. She protected her, too, from the truth of what had motivated it.

'One night, when Fanny was about ten or eleven years old, she stole downstairs from her bedroom because she'd left her favourite doll in the kitchen. She heard a rumble of men's voices in the front parlour, which the mammy had kept closed to her, saying it was the place where she earned them the money to keep 'em fed and clothed.

'Her little-girl mind was thrilled by the notion of masculinity in her house. She peeped though the keyhole. The mammy was entertaining two men — big fellows, drinking hard liquor, smoking strong cigars, talking men's talk and doing strange things to the mammy she'd never seen done before.

'More, when the pair were done with the woman, they got to talking about Fanny's family and their deaths.'

Jackson pictured a tiny Fanny in a

long flannel nightgown, her reddish hair braided and in bows, her doll tucked under her arm, fascinated by adults' pleasure-taking, listening to the true story of her own unfortunate life.

Lil carried on. 'Well, as these men told it and the mammy didn't deny, it seemed the stinking white soldiers who'd brought down the wrath of the Indians on the heads of Fanny's ma and pa and brothers were led by a Lieutenant Ezra Creede — a rake-hell who was the guiltiest and wickedest of the lot. Through the night, drunk on rum, he'd raped and killed several Cheyenne maidens and gotten clean away with it.

'Though Fanny scarce understood what she'd heard, she kept the details in her young mind, where they preyed on her thinking, making her the rather strange person she was.'

Lil paused for breath.

Jackson said, 'You know I'm beginning to get a line now on what happened. Belated retribution. But

225

killing the man . . . that seems kind of out of keeping for a woman like Fanny.'

Lil had the answer for his doubt.

'On the night of the ball at Fort Dennis, Fanny was considerably influenced by an excess of strong drink. She was already full of hatred for Major Creede, knowing the true blame for her family's destruction was his. All the cruelty and injustice he stood for came to a head — plumb unhinged her mind — when he spanked me. She could see the truth for herself: Creede still had a taste for torrid little games.

'And he went ahead and proved it, sealed his fate, when he later cornered Fanny.

'She'd argued with Tom and gone off alone into some dark corner. Creede made a proposition requiring retirement to the privacy of his quarters. Fanny, emboldened by drink, agreed. She reckoned to seize the opportunity both to disappoint Creede and give him a scathing tongue-lashing.

'But she didn't want to get a

spanking, so she 'borrowed' the dagger and took it along for the defence of her honour. In the event, Creede quickly overpowered her, giving her the bruises everyone afterwards supposed she'd gotten from her husband.

'She stabbed Creede mortally while he was in the act of raping her.

'Panic! She had a notion her story wouldn't be believed. Creede's boss, General Morgan, was an old hand at covering up and she'd surely be hanged. Fanny and Tom Kennedy sought me out, and we quickly hatched a scheme to save her neck.

'I'd draw the attention to me, because I was the one best able to lead the hunt for the culprit on a wild-goose chase. As soon as they could, and with suspicion diverted, the Kennedys would quit Fort Dennis and head for a fresh start somewhere in the South Seas. A written confession by Fanny to the murder would be left, wrapped in oilcloth and hidden under a rock. I'd later recover it and send it to Colonel or

Mrs Lexborough. With Fanny and her husband long fled, sailing across the ocean with new identities, the letter would leave me free to reclaim my life.'

Jackson shook his head. 'What a loco, harebrained scheme! To think it almost worked.'

'It *would* have worked,' Lil said indignantly, 'if the Kennedys hadn't tried to take a trail through the canyons and lost their horses and themselves.'

'I can think of one big loophole you've over-looked, Lil Goodnight.'

'Oh! And what's that?'

Jackson sighed. 'Mike Covington isn't the only one who's a stickler for the rules. There'll be folks who'll insist on charging you as an accessory if the full story comes out.'

Lil blanched. 'You mean, they'll send me to the pen?'

'Well, I don't know they'll push it that far. But maybe you should hide out a while longer and let me retrieve this exonerating letter. When the truth comes out, it might be best if no one were to know you already knew it — let alone that you tried to mislead the investigation by framing yourself and hightailing it to establish your guilt. Better to let everyone think you cut and run in fear when the folks at the ball jumped to the conclusion you must be Creede's killer.'

'Do you think they'll believe Fanny had it in her to frame anyone?'

Jackson shrugged. 'They do say beneath red hair lies guile and snare . . . We'll have to chance whether they'll swallow it. You took a far bigger gamble when you jumped into the whole crazy affair as a kind of willing scapegoat.'

'Sure, but it seemed a worthwhile gamble. Besides, I was already in the ruckus in a way. I wanted my own back on that skunk Creede and I didn't see why anybody should suffer for his death. I feel damn sorry Fanny and Kennedy didn't make it through the trouble like I'd planned.'

Jackson and Lil shared a moment's sad silence, thinking on it with regret.

Then Jackson gestured emptily. 'At least they're together forever now.'

Lil agreed this was so. 'Fanny got awful tired with army life, specially when Tom was away. They argued about it often. Now Fanny will never go again to an unshared bed in Fort Dennis. She won't have to toss and turn, the lonely nights all passing slow, while her husband is off in some dangerous place doing his duty as a soldier.'

'That's a good thought, Lil,' Jackson said.

But she was wistful when he rode away with the battle-fatigued troopers.

'Have *you* ever been lonely?' was a question he hadn't thought to ask Misfit Lil.

THE END

HELL'S COURTYARD

Cobra Sunman

Indian Territory, popularly called Hell's Courtyard, was where bad men fled to escape the law. Buck Rogan, a deputy marshal hunting the killer Jed Calder, found the trail leading into Hell's Courtyard and went after his quarry, finding every man's hand against him. Rogan was also searching for the hideout of Jake Yaris, an outlaw running most of the lawlessness directed at Kansas and Arkansas. Single-minded and capable, Rogan would fight the bad men to the last desperate shot.

SARATOGA

Jim Lawless

Pinkerton operative Temple Bywater arrives in Saratoga, Wyoming facing a mystery: who murdered Senator Andrew Stone? Was it his successor, Nathan Wedge? Or were lawyers Forrest and Millard Jackson, and Marshal Tom Gaines involved? Bywater, along with his sidekick Clarence Sugg, and Texas Jack Logan, faces gunmen whose allegiances are unknown. The showdown comes in Saratoga. Will he come out on top in a bloody gun fight against an adversary who is not only tough, but also completely unforeseen?

PEACE AT ANY PRICE

Chap O'Keefe

Jim Hunter and Matt Harrison's Double H ranch thrived . . . till their crew marched away to war's glory, and outlaws destroyed everything and murdered oldster Walt Burridge. When the war ended, the two Hs started over. However, for Jim, war had wrought changes beyond endurance. So Jim rode out and into the arms of his wartime love, the gun-running adventuress Lena-Marie Baptiste. Now, trapped by his vow to avenge Old Walt, he must choose between enmity and love, life and death.